THIS BAND WILL SAVE YOUR LIFE

This Band Will Save Your Life is a work of fiction. The characters, incidents, and dialogue are drawn from the author's imagination and are not to be construed as real. Any resemblance to actual events or persons, living or dead, is entirely coincidental.

Copyright © 2022 by Willis Adler

All rights reserved. Except as permitted under the U.S. Copyright Act of 1976, no part of this publication may be reproduced or used in any manner whatsoever without the express written permission of the publisher except for the use of brief quotations in a book review.

Printed in the United States of America

First Printing, 2022

ISBN 978-0-578-34345-7

For my friend, Geoff. I think you would have really liked this book (while also still finding a way to make fun of me for writing it).

For BP3. I wrote the first sentence the day we lost you. You were with me the entire time.

And for W, who helped me find my way out of the dark. I miss you every day.

THIS BAND WILL SAVE YOUR LIFE

WILLIS ADLER

PROLOGUE

She had no idea how long she'd been running, but she knew she was about to give up, even if that meant she was going to die.

She kept telling herself it was just a bear, but deep down she knew it was something else. Something much worse.

It had been Dylan's idea to drive out to the woods in the first place. He'd asked her pull off on the access road and park so they could take the long, slow walk down to the lake together. She thought it was sweet at the time, but now she felt like an entirely different person than the one who'd made that decision.

She knew what he was going to do before he even started. He was giving her his great big final argument about why they should stay together, and she let him go on for a while before her mind drifted off. She'd appreciated it, of course, because who doesn't want to be wanted? But she'd made up her mind long ago and thought it would be easier to let graduation do all the heavy lifting. High school was almost done, and they were going off to opposite ends of the country. She was ready to tear open the packaging on her brand-new life, and she didn't want anything tethering her to home. Their time was over.

She was counting stars when it killed him. One second he was earnestly extolling the virtues of dating long-distance, and the next he was gurgling and bleeding all over the front of the light gray Patagonia zip-up she'd bought him last Christmas.

His throat had been ripped out.

She thought it was a cruel joke at first—as if he knew she was going to dump him and was mad enough to hurt her with a prank. She couldn't process what she was seeing. She'd never seen so much blood in her entire life. She didn't have time to be sad about it; as soon as she realized he was dying for real, that thing stood up on its hind legs, dragged Dylan down to the ground, and started feasting on him.

That was when she took off.

She waved her key fob overhead, double-pressed the lock button for the millionth time, and finally heard the far-off honk. Her car was close enough to give her a small spark of hope.

She kept pressing the button and following the horn, even as a small, dark storm cloud in the back of her mind warned her she was letting that thing know exactly where she was headed. But once she burst into the clearing and saw her bright red Subaru, it was the last thing on her mind.

She sprinted to the driver's side and yanked the door as hard as she could. She was confused for a second when it didn't give, until she realized that she'd been pushing the *lock* button for the last five minutes and she hadn't actually unlocked it yet.

She opened the door, dove into the front seat, pulled the door shut behind her, then hammered the lock down with her fist as if the act itself somehow made her safer. There was nothing but the sound of her rapid, shallow breathing before she jammed the key into the ignition and fired up the engine.

The headlights sliced through the darkness. She stared out the windshield, even though she was terrified to do it. She saw nothing but spruce trees and wide-open road in front of her.

There was a *ping* as her phone connected with her car's Bluetooth. Her first impulse was to call her dad.

He picked up on the second ring. She started sobbing the second she heard him say "Hellllllo…" in the familiar sing-songy way he'd done her enter life. She told him what was happening, and he told her to drive, to get out of the woods as fast as possible, that it was all going to be okay. And she believed him. But when she put her car into gear and smashed down on the gas, the car didn't move an inch. The tires screamed and smoked and kicked up mounds of dead pine needles, but the vehicle never left that spot.

Until something started dragging it back into the woods.

Her father listened as she screamed for the last time she ever would.

Then the silence stretched on long enough for him to pull the phone away from his ear to make sure the call was still connected.

It was.

And he was still listening when the thing on the other end began to eat his daughter.

1

Connor Quikstadt woke up 15 minutes late on his last day of high school.

He was still up a solid two hours earlier than every other kid his age would be that morning, but it didn't matter. He instantly felt cobwebs of nervous energy form in the back of his mind. He had way too much to do.

Connor padded down the carpeted hallway. The faint glow of early morning bled through the curtains just enough that he didn't bother flipping on the overhead light.

He took another step closer to it. The biggest moment in his day for the past five years; a special kind of maniacal joke, where the only thing he looked forward to happened within the first few minutes of waking up. It was his one flicker of unbridled hope, despite the fact that deep down he was terrified that the answer to the question would always be the same, no matter how many times he asked it.

Sam's room.

The door was slightly open, just like he'd left it last night. And despite knowing it was going to happen long before it did, he still couldn't stop his breath from catching in his throat as he passed the frame and leaned into the room.

The lights were off, and the bed was made and empty. There were no signs of life other than the ones he maintained, just like every single other morning for the past five years.

There was always tomorrow.

Connor drifted back out into the hall and into the bathroom. He stared at his sandy-brown mess of bedhead in the mirror. He'd definitely gotten that from Mom. But the rest of him was all Dad.

He squeezed a glob of toothpaste onto his toothbrush and let his mind wander along the usual route: Sam and Dad somewhere together, bumping elbows playfully as they brushed their teeth. They'd have a laugh as they both leaned in to spit at the same time, but then Dad would insist that Sam go first. That was just the type of Dad he was.

Connor turned on the shower, stepped into an underwhelming stream of tepid water, and lathered up. Muscle memory took over as he imagined all the possible different lives Sam and Dad could be leading right now: crab fishing in Alaska, flipping pizzas in New York, surfing in Hawaii. Or maybe Dad finally got his wish and they were reffing youth hockey together in some speck-on-the-map town way up in the frozen tundra of Northern Canada.

But no matter how many lives he imagined or how many times he shampooed, there was one hurdle he never seemed to get past: why they had left in the first place.

And why they had never come back.

-

Connor stood outside of Sam's room again. It used to be that of a semi-normal teenage boy…until *that summer*.

He still got pissed when he thought about it. It wasn't just that Sam got to stay with their grandparents in Berkeley, California for *three* whole months while Connor was stuck at home. It was that when Sam came back, he was a completely different person. He had changed.

Sam had a summer full of big city adventures with their cool older cousin Billie, and suddenly, even though the three-year age gap between Sam and Connor was still the same, it felt like they were a million years apart. Sam had grown up. And in the process, he'd grown right past all the things he and Connor loved doing together, like collecting baseball cards, reading *Goosebumps* books, playing Mario Kart, and watching stupid action movies. Sam had shoved all that stuff into the bottom of his closet and forgotten about it like it never mattered to him in the first place. Connor felt like he was down there too, relegated to the closet floor with the rest of the things Sam didn't care about anymore.

After *that summer*, there was only one thing that mattered to Sam. One thing that was *the* most important thing in the entire world. It covered his walls, invaded his brain, and he never, ever shut up about it.

Heatseeker.

Heatseeker was some band Billie convinced Sam to see by sneaking out the second-story window of their grandparent's house in the middle of the night. They played at a skeezy punk club called 924 Gilman Street. They were young, loud and snotty; Sam said he'd never heard anything like them in his entire life. They were instantly his favorite band, his first favorite band, and first loves got the gift of your entire heart.

But there was something weird about Heatseeker, something Connor couldn't understand no matter how many times Sam tried to explain it: they didn't exist—at least, as far as Connor could tell. He'd Googled them a thousand times, in a thousand different ways, but it didn't matter.

There wasn't anything about them anywhere online.

No music existed; no pictures, no videos…not even a Bandcamp site. Nothing. There were just a bunch of links to a song called "Heatseeker" by AC/DC (and no, Sam most certainly did not like AC/DC); a Wikipedia page for a Transformer named Heatseeker; and apparently, a movie called *Heatseeker* released in 1995, probably straight-to-video, about a kickboxing champion who had to fight cyborgs in order to get his fiancée back—which, pre-*that summer*, Sam would have been all over.

But none of that mattered. Sam was adamant. He knew what he'd seen, and he was smitten.

Soon, all of Sam's old Mariners and Canucks posters had been torn from the walls and replaced by hand-drawn pictures of the band. Because what do you do when your favorite band in the entire world doesn't have any posters or pictures of themselves? Sam decided to make his own.

They were laughable at first—at least, Connor would laugh at them, purely out of spite. But that didn't sway Sam. He'd spent hours in his room, drawing away, until eventually all his dedication paid off and he got really, really good.

Sam's last batch of pictures was exceptional. The first one was a logo: 12-inch-tall letters, an *H* and an *S*, pressed against each other in the center of a badass shield. Sam taped that one to the wall right above his headboard. The second was a close-up of the guitar player's 1964 Sunburst Fender Stratocaster; Connor would never forget the specific year and model, because Sam had only mentioned it, like, fourteen million times. And Sam was so proud of the third drawing that he put it in an 8x10 frame he'd bought at The Dollar Jamboree and hung it on the wall like a proper work of art— a full-on, mid-song action shot of all four members of the band playing together onstage.

Connor loved the framed band shot the most. It was not only his favorite, but also probably the best drawing he'd ever seen that had been created by someone he actually knew. Every time he looked at it now, he wished he'd told Sam that, at least once.

While Sam's wall was comprised of ninety percent Heatseeker drawings, the last ten was taken up by his 1972 Hagstrom HIIN-OT guitar. When Sam came back from *that summer* all body-snatchered out about loud music, Dad couldn't have been more excited. He himself must have been body-snatchered at some point, too. One Saturday, he came home with a guitar case. He'd found it at a garage sale, on the cheap, most likely because it was busted; the wiring was jacked, and it was missing a huge chunk of wood from the back of the neck. But it became his thing with Sam. Every weekend, the two of them would take the Hagstrom out to the garage and mess with it until Mom yelled at them to come in and eat something. Once, they even got it to let out an angry screech of ungodly feedback while it was plugged into Sam's mini Fender Deluxe amp. Mom would always ask them how much longer until it might actually work, and Dad would lean back in his chair, smile and say they were *this close* while doing the whole fingers-almost-touching thing.

Connor slowly lifted the Hagstrom out of its wall mount, being extra-careful with the neck, and set it softly on Sam's bed. He wiped it down methodically with an old piece of torn t-shirt like he'd done a hundred other times. Then he secured it back up on the wall. He deliberately flipped the piece of t-shirt over in his hand to ensure it was clean-side-up, then wiped down everything else in Sam's room until it was spic, span, and raring to go. He stared at the room full of his brother's possessions. Every single thing that mattered most to Sam in the entire world was all just sitting there, waiting for him to come back.

Connor flicked on the lights as he strolled into the kitchen, his favorite room in the house. Memories awaited him there, too. Once Dad acquired the Hagstrom, he could probably sense, as any good dad would have, that he needed to carve out some quality time for Connor as well. That was when *Ultimate Breakfast!* was born. Connor could still hear the cheesy, mock-superhero voice Dad used to announce it. He was never sure why Dad had started saying it that way, but it didn't matter; Connor just loved that he did. It was one of the things he missed the most.

For the six months before Sam and Dad disappeared, every *Ultimate Breakfast!* week would unfold in the same way:

Monday and Tuesday: Connor and Dad did deep individual research to come up with some kind of insane breakfast concoction to attempt.

Wednesday: They compared notes and selected their challenge.

Thursday: Dad drove them all to Finer Foods Grocery on Lake Street (the nicer one) to purchase ingredients and a super-secret candy bar for each of them that they would never tell Mom about.

Friday night: **Prep work.**
Saturday morning: Chaos reigned. *Ultimate Breakfast!* ensued.

For their last *Ultimate Breakfast!* they'd made a spinach, egg and white cheddar quiche, complete with a crust from scratch. They'd both agreed it was easily the best thing they'd made thus far. Chock full of confidence, they'd decided they were finally ready to tackle the ridiculous Cap'n Crunch-battered French toast recipe they'd been sitting on…but then Dad told Connor they'd have to push it back a week, since he and Sam had something important to do on the following Saturday morning. Of course, Connor's feelings were hurt. He hadn't spoken a word to either Sam or Dad for the next two days. And then, they left.

And they never came back.

So while the last day of high school would typically call for a breakfast as *Ultimate!* as possible, all Connor really wanted today was something to eat.

He poked his head into the fridge and selected his weapons of choice. He set out four eggs. He'd learned he could poach eggs in the microwave by filling a coffee mug with a half-cup of water and a pinch of salt. He'd crack the egg in, cover the top of the mug with a small plate, smash the one-minute express button on the microwave, and voila—a perfectly serviceable poach. Where he refused to cut corners, however, was the toast. There was only one way to do toast. Dad taught him that. "First of all," he'd said, "if you don't have good bread, you're donezo. Next, get the toaster screaming hot. Hot as it can go. Some infrared toasters get up to 750 degrees Fahrenheit. That's hot enough to melt lead. Two-and-a-half to three minutes in one of those bad boys and the outside crisps up without drying out the middle. Crunchy outside; soft inside. Use the best butter you can find. Like anything you cook, it should be seasoned. So hit it with salt. Then lastly, and maybe most important, eat it as fast as you can get it in your face. Because no matter how good the bread is or how hot the toaster, every piece of toast will get soggy eventually." So that was how he did it, every single time.

Once he'd finished eating his breakfast, Connor padded back down the hallway carrying a tray of food. There was some lukewarm coffee in a *Dad To Bee!* mug that had a picture of a smiling bee on it; two poached eggs of the microwaved variety; and two pieces of buttered toast, sliced diagonally, that had long since gone soggy. But it didn't really matter; they probably wouldn't get eaten anyway.

He paused momentarily outside the door to his parent's room, feeling foolish for even contemplating whether to knock. He hip-checked the door open and stepped in softly.

She was in the same place as always: the recliner. Sitting in the same position as always: knees pulled up and hidden somewhere inside Dad's old varsity hockey jersey while facing away from Connor, staring out the window.

Connor cleared his throat. "Hey, Mom."

She didn't move.

Connor tried to remember the last time he'd seen her face, but he couldn't. It had been that long. He could walk over, stand directly in front of her, and force her to look at him if he wanted to. But what would be the point? It wouldn't change anything. And while he felt terrible for thinking it, there was a part of him that got a little more scared everyday about what she was beginning to look like: someone without anything in the middle anymore. A ghost.

He continued quietly and carefully, as if the volume of his voice might wound her. "Today is my last day of high school, so I'll be home pretty much all the time from now. At least until I figure out a job."

She exhaled slowly. At least she was breathing. Then she croaked out softly, "That's nice, Connor."

Connor moved toward the corner of the bed and replaced the mostly-full dinner tray he'd left her last night with the currently-full breakfast tray from this morning.

"I'm leaving, so I'll start the movie for you."

Her attention remained focused out the window.

Connor headed for the TV at the foot of the bed and grabbed the DVD on top of the TV stand. *The Breakfast Club*. The story went that Dad and Mom had gone to see it for their very first date back in high school. Afterward, Dad said there was no possible way they'd ever see a better date movie, so they probably shouldn't bother going to romantic movies together ever again. The man might have been a genius. It had been their movie ever since.

Connor hit play.

By the time Brian Johnson said "Dear Mr. Vernon" over static shots of Shermer High, he was long gone.

2

Connor sat on the curb, staring back at his house as he waited for Nina and her mom to come out from next door. His house had been beautiful once—shiny and new, and someone gazed at it with eyes full of longing and promise.

But that was a long time ago.

It was a squat, single-level ranch on the south side of Evergreen, Washington. Years ago, someone had decided to call the neighborhood Ballast Point to make it sound more cosmopolitan and hopefully lure a few families into moving back. But it didn't end up fooling anyone. Evergreen was a fishing town first and foremost, but when the fish dried up, so did the people. In the '60s and '70s it had been the kind of idyllic small town people disappeared to, until suddenly one day it became a place that people disappeared from. Sometimes overnight. Now, Connor thought it was mostly just sad. As every teenage kid has lamented in every small town ever, nothing really seemed to happen there.

Connor loved their house growing up, though. It was full of warmth and laughter, food and music, and was his own personal safety zone. Now, it was just a rapidly-aging pile of brick, wood and shingles that needed its shutters replaced, and for someone to figure out what to do with the front yard. He noticed even more of the blue paint flaking off the sides—New Providence Navy, to be specific. Mom had made a huge deal out of the name when she brought home the six cans of paint one day in the middle of summer 2008. The name was what had sold her on it, she'd said, and their house was desperately in need of a fresh look. Sam and Connor had both been enlisted for the job, despite their multitude of protests. Plans were hatched, brushes were cleaned, and many a drop cloth was unrolled.

But nobody bothered to tell the weather.

It rained every single day for the entire next week—non-stop, all day long. But the nights were clear and full of stars. So after the eighth day of rain in a row, Mom decided she'd had enough.

They would paint at night.

As ridiculous as the entire thing was—painting by flashlight, with the radio down just low enough that the neighbors wouldn't complain—it was probably a lot better than being out in the sun all day. Plus, it made for a much better story.

That was also the summer that Dave Koralik, the weird, lanky kid who lived up the street, drove a Mr. Tastee ice cream truck. His boss didn't want him coming back with old inventory, so one night he stopped by on his way home and offered to unload it all to Mom for a measly five bucks. Connor was surprised by how much more willing he was to stay up and paint once he'd pounded four crunch bars, two creamsicles, and a bomb pop in the span of two hours. Dave stopped by the next three nights as well, supplying treats and re-upping their sugar high while they finished all the work.

What Mom didn't know was that underneath the topcoat of New Providence Navy there was a litany of dirty words hidden in the coats below. Every time she'd step inside for a bathroom break or to refill the pitcher of iced tea, Sam and Connor would one-up each other by painting the most ridiculous thing they could think of on the side of the house, posturing like they intended to leave it there, then inevitably painting over it as fast as possible before she came back out and busted them. It would've been a lot more daring if not for the cover of night, but they were both of the proper age that it amused them to no end, and helped to pass the time. While Connor was super-proud of his "Fang Boner," he had to admit that Sam had taken the trophy easily when he came up with "Butthole University."

Connor's reverie faded as the Veseley's front door opened and Nina and Mrs. Veseley strode out on to their porch. Connor heard Nina saying, "Mom, that's some monumental bullsh—"

Mrs. Veseley pinched her daughter's lips closed before she could finish. "First of all, Nina: language. Secondly: no one is forcing you to take your grandmother's five-hundred-dollar graduation check. You're more than welcome to give it back. Her birthday party is tonight. You can't take her money with one hand and blow off her birthday with the other. So that's the end of it."

Mrs. Veseley weaved around to the driver's side of their sporty-yet-sensible Volvo wagon. She saw Connor approaching and gave him a megawatt smile. "Well, good morning there, Mr. Man! Last day as a Wildcat...don't you look handsome!"

But Nina was not easily deterred. "Grandma is a hundred million years old. Not only is her party guaranteed to be super-lame, but if it isn't over before ten, I'll be amazed. Don't make me give up my entire night. Most of my friend's parties don't start until late anyway. I'll do Grandma's for an hour, then I bail. Deal?"

Mrs. Veseley sighed in exasperation and rubbed her forehead. Nina had her on the ropes.

"These are my last few high school parties," Nina reminded her. "I'll probably never see some of those people ever again."

Mrs. Veseley looked at Connor. "Are you going to any of these parties tonight?"

Connor shook his head adamantly. "I can't *wait* to never see some of those people ever again."

Before Mrs. Veseley could even get the "I'll talk it over with your father" out of her mouth, Nina already knew she'd won.

The three of them opened their car doors, practically in unison, and slid into their respective ranks. Nina offered up a cursory glance toward Connor in the backseat. "Last day of high school, Quikstuff. Better buckle up." Nina was the only one who still called him that. It was the result of an unfortunate mispronunciation by a substitute teacher in fourth grade that had stuck. Connor felt like he'd dodged a major bullet though, by narrowly avoiding "Quikstud" instead. The enthusiasm for it had dwindled significantly over the years, but for whatever reason Nina still held fast.

Connor suddenly realized that no one might ever call him that again after today.

He had known Nina since he was four and she was three-and-a-half. Her family had moved in next door, coming all the way from Dayton, Ohio, after her father decided he'd had enough of the "goddamned snow" and traded it in for buckets of rain instead. They liked Washington well enough though, and it seemed to suit them. When she was younger, Nina had been painfully shy, and not simply in a new-kid way. It went on for years. Then one day, the dam suddenly burst, and she hadn't shut up about much since. It was as if she'd spent all those years listening and quietly compiling a master list of counterpoints. She would talk back to anyone, anywhere, at any time. She was fearless. And that specific skill set had cast her toward one of the few designated roles typically held by teenage girls who refused to stop running their mouths: being a gossip, a rebel, or a terribly annoying, brown-nosing know-it-all.

Connor was glad that Nina had chosen to rebel.

He figured a lot of that had to do with Sam. While Nina barely tolerated Connor, she cared about Sam in a way she would remember for the rest of her life. Connor didn't want to discount it as something as simple as puppy love; it had been full of admiration, and a lot more real than that. When Sam came back body-snatched after that summer, it seemed as if he'd transmitted it to Nina as well. As soon as Sam got into music, Nina did too.

It was probably just about impressing Sam at first. She would angle her Bluetooth speaker out her bedroom window and blast as loud as possible whatever crappy, obscure, droning indie band of the moment she could find, in hopes that Sam would notice. One time,

Connor actually liked one of the songs enough to ask her who sang it, but she had no idea who it was

A few years later it had taken hold for real, and after that came the vintage t-shirts, skater shoes, hair dye and Army jackets. Now, Nina had a whole rotating squad of burnouts and weirdo music kids she hung out with on the constant. She was their fearless leader.

Connor knew she'd taken it really hard when Sam disappeared. It tore through a part of her heart in the same way it had torn through his. He could feel that. He'd given her one of Sam's Heatseeker drawings a few weeks after he went missing, an early version of the shield logo, and a few days later Nina came to school with a patch she'd made out of the drawing sewn on to the left shoulder of her jacket. She'd had two more jackets since, each one covered in all kinds of patches and buttons, but Heatseeker was the only patch to show up on all three, as far as Connor could tell.

Connor stared out the window as Evergreen passed by. For better or worse, it was his town, the only place he'd ever really known. Deep down he was fine with that; he'd known for a long time that he would end up stuck there. Someone had to take care of his mom and their house. There was no one to do it but him. He didn't really have anything better to do anyway.

Most people would probably have balked at that. He was so young…he had so much life to live and so many things to see and do. But none of that felt true. He'd never once thought about going to college, or what he might really like to do once he grew up. He'd never been given the option to even consider those things, so eventually he just grew bored and rudderless. He was going to have to get a job now, but the specifics of that weren't important to him— just something that paid decent money and preferably had nothing to do with fast food. His Grandpa Frank used to say, "Can't have big dreams if they got no place to grow." Connor always liked that. So that was how he would explain his situation if anyone ever bothered to ask.

He watched Mrs. Veseley in the front seat, her hands cemented on the steering wheel at 10 and 2. They were always this way; she was a real stickler for the rules of the road like that. Her head drifted softly from side to side rhythmically, a tiny habit she'd developed while driving over the years, something she probably didn't even realize she was doing. Connor had grown to depend on her a lot. There was a large part of him that was worried about how much he was going to miss seeing her every morning. He had contracted a very significant case of Mom Envy over the last few years. Mrs. Veseley was a straight-shooter, a trait he had grown to appreciate after countless conversations with patronizing adults who feigned concern about him and his missing brother and dad. She was also incredibly kind and thoughtful. Every once in a while, she would "accidentally" pack an extra lunch or have too many "dang" leftovers to finish herself, and she'd give them to Connor. Somehow, it was always right when he needed it the most, too, as if her mom sense started tingling and she just knew. It was a tiny gesture from the universe to pick him up, dust him off and gently nudge him forward every time.

He decided right then that she would go down in his official record book as his second-most favorite person to ever drive him to school.

The history of Connor's morning commutes to school went as follows: Mom drove him from preschool through third grade; she was the worst, and had absolutely no patience for any other driver ever, honking her horn like she got paid to do it. Then Dad drove him from third grade through eighth; he wasn't quite as bad as Mom, but man, did he love to ride that brake. He also insisted on always keeping the heat on, regardless of the temperature outside, and sometimes that, mixed with all the brake-riding starts and stops, would make Connor super nauseous. And after that came the pinnacle of his various journeys to academia: Sam got his license. It was six of the most glorious weeks of his life—six weeks of loud music and no parents. And there were Pop Tarts. Sam kept two boxes in the glovebox at all times. One was whatever new, disgusting, pumpkin-spiced or blue raspberry flavor they were peddling that week; Sam liked to be adventurous with his junk food. The other was always maple and brown sugar—the best—because he knew they were Connor's all-time favorite. That was the kind of big brother he was, and Connor knew it was rare.

After Sam and Dad disappeared, Connor walked to school for a bit. Then one day, Nina and Mrs. Veseley saw him, pulled over, and absorbed him into their routine. They'd kept it this way ever since. A much bigger gesture from the universe, perhaps.

Something on Nina's phone made her to squirm excitedly in the front seat. She dialed with a fury, then jammed the phone to her ear. "The Black Hole tonight? You're sure? Because if you're messing with me right now I'm gonna do horrible things to your entire family." She squealed, kicked her legs and proceeded to lose every ounce of her sanity. "Why the hell, of all the places in the entire world, would they come play Nowheresville Evergreen in the middle of the woods at the freaking Black Hole where the sound sucks and the drinks are ridiculously overpriced…"

Nina sensed her mom's sudden glare.

"…for soda, because all we drink is soda and they charge so much for soda."

Mrs. Veseley didn't buy it for a second.

"Dude," Nina continued, "it doesn't matter. I don't even care why they're here. All I know is we're going, and I can't believe it's actually happening. We're going to see Heatseeker tonight, and I don't care if I ever go to another show again after that for the rest of my entire life."

Heatseeker.

Connor's breath stopped for a full five seconds.

3

The rest of the drive was a blur in which Nina seemed to text every single person on Earth who had a phone while Connor became lost in thought in the backseat. Heatseeker was playing somewhere in Evergreen tonight. Did Sam know somehow? Would he be there? Connor knew if Sam was anywhere within a thousand-mile radius, there was no possible way he'd miss it.

Before Connor realized it they were stopped in front of Westerberg High School, and Nina had already sprinted from the car. Connor leaned in from the back, halfway between the two front seats. He wanted to tell Mrs. Veseley just how much all the rides and accidental extra lunches had meant to him. How some days her warm smile and hokey greetings were the most interaction he'd have with another person the entire day. How she'd kept him going, and how much he was going to miss her. But all that squeaked out was a simple, "Thanks for all the rides, Mrs. Veseley."

She smiled. "We're only a door away, Connor. You're welcome anytime."

Connor stepped out and watched until her Volvo wagon completely disappeared from sight.

Then he took the front stairs up two at a time and headed right into the belly of the beast.

-

Connor had made up his mind about high school a long time ago. He knew that for some kids, it would be the best time of their lives, formative years that overflowed with golden memories of best friends and time spent figuring out the answers to life's big questions: who you wanted to be, who you wanted to love you—or to like you (which were completely different things), and what you wanted to do with the rest of your life. For these kids, high school was everything everyone had always portended it would be: the last beautiful chapter in the book of growing up.

For others kids, it was something much different: a nightmare hellscape of strangers who looked right through you—or, even worse, had judged you immediately and decided you were unworthy. It was cold shoulders and whispers that cut through to the bone. Those kids never forget what high school felt like, and as they moved on through life the fact that they'd survived was a badge of courage they brandished for everyone to see.

But for most kids, high school was just more school. A way station between the extremes. The place where they were stuck for far too long every day, counting the seconds until they could sprint out the front door and into the sunshine to go do whatever actually made them happy in life. It was the great precursor to growing up and having to work for a living.

For Connor, it was closest to this, a place full of things he was obligated to do. He'd floated through without leaving much of a mark on anything in the building. The thing about having your brother and your father disappear when you were 13 years old, Connor knew, was that you no longer carried the emotional bandwidth to care about things that didn't *really* matter anymore. So crushes, popularity, parties, who drove what car or who was jealous of whose girlfriend—it was all just background noise to him. He missed out on the crucial and specific details in the great conversation that was high school.

As Connor stood at his locker and watched all his classmates skitter back and forth to pen heartfelt "Keep in touch!" or "I'll never forget you!" messages in one another's yearbooks, he couldn't help but feel a twinge of sadness. The circus was packing up and leaving town, and even though he'd always told himself he didn't want to go, now it was officially too late to ever buy a ticket.

He noticed Danielle Gutter walking toward him, carrying two yearbooks. Danielle was one of the rare people who seemed to have been born knowing exactly who they were. She'd been virtually the same girl since kindergarten, while most of their classmates had tried on new personalities like outfits. She was chubby and awkward but well-read, viciously intelligent and self-confident to the brink of arrogance, no matter how much the pressure of social acceptance had tried to erode it away.

She stopped in front of Connor's locker.

"Hey Connor," Danielle said. "Remember Chase Heffernan?"

Connor nodded. "Skater kid who got expelled for taking upper-deckers in Principal Yseabart's private bathroom. I still can't believe it took them six months to catch him."

Danielle held out one of the yearbooks. "Want this? His parents pre-paid at the beginning of the year. I DM'ed him to see if he wanted to come pick it up, but I'm pretty sure he doesn't since he told me, very specifically, how he thought I should attempt to fornicate with myself."

It was a legitimately nice gesture, and Connor wished he could just take it as that, but he could tell she felt sorry for him in the same way most of his other classmates did. The specific way in which they pitied him yet also felt incredibly relieved that they weren't him at the exact same time. It was all he could see in her eyes. Just another side effect of Sam and Dad, and a sting that hadn't lessened over time.

But he took the yearbook anyway.

"Thanks, Danielle."

She waited awkwardly, assuming he was going to ask her to sign it. But he simply placed into his backpack, then zipped it up and sealed it away inside.

He walked off down the hall by himself, without the idea that Danielle had wanted him to sign her yearbook ever even being a possibility in his mind.

It wasn't until lunch that Connor finally got the chance to talk to Nina. She was sitting at her usual table in the back corner of the cafeteria, holding court with all the other misfit toys. Connor hated the cafeteria. There was a permanent stink in the air, like something had crawled into the deep fryer and died. He typically ate lunch in the library, where he'd lose track of time using the X-Plane Regional flight simulator on one of the taxpayer-purchased 17-inch Macbook Pros. He had asked Mrs. Rexford, the head librarian, if they could upgrade to X-Plane Global about a hundred times, but she repeatedly shot him down; no one ever used it but him. With today being the last day of school, he figured his chances were officially cooked. Maybe he would pick it up himself whenever he got his first real paycheck. That way he could at least go out and see what the rest of the computer-generated world had to offer.

His attention was drawn back to Nina. Her hands oscillated wildly as she blasted through rapid fire talking points to the rest of her lunch table. As he closed in, he could hear her recounting the moment she found out about the Heatseeker show, down to the exact microsecond. Connor plopped down on to the bench across from her.

The conversation stopped immediately.

He was seated between Fragile Dave and Faraz Pinter. Fragile Dave had earned his unfortunate nickname after he made the mistake of crying for three days in a row during the fetal pig dissection portion of eighth-grade biology and Mr. Hoover asked him if he was too fragile to complete the dissection in front of their entire class. Connor always thought that was a serious dick move—even more so for a teacher—but as Fragile Dave glared at him now and made an extra obvious show of rolling his eyes, Connor didn't feel so bad about it anymore.

"What up, Con Air?" Faraz said. He didn't miss a beat as he held his fist out, waiting patiently for Connor to bump it. Faraz was a tiny, nebbish, hyper-mouthed Indian American kid who somehow ended up with all the music weirdos, mostly because he didn't fit in particularly well anywhere else. They had adopted him as their own, and he was happy enough to enjoy the security that this pack mentality provided. It also didn't hurt that after his parents were divorced, his dad bought a tricked-out bachelor pad in the bougie Northwest section of Evergreen and was frequently out of town. He was one of the few kids who never treated Connor like he was different. Connor wondered sometimes if Faraz even knew about Sam and his Dad. In a weird way, it kind of made Connor like him even more.

Connor finally bumped fists with Faraz and glanced across the table toward Bailey Harper, who was essentially Nina's glorified bodyguard. He needed to make sure he would have time to plead his case. If Bailey was bothered at all by Connor's presence, he didn't show it. Bailey was a gigantic hulk who used to play football and had been a legit redneck until he was ridiculed one too many times for having two girls' first names for his entire name. He cracked and became pseudo-goth. Connor was pretty sure Bailey had been smoking unfiltered Lucky Strike cigarettes since the sixth grade; he always kept a pack rolled up in his shirt sleeve like some wayward S.E. Hinton character. He was also absolutely sure Bailey's father had been arrested for burglary four times. With a resume like that, his place at this table was practically predestined.

Noticeably absent was Marissa Spooner, Nina's best friend, and that was fine with Connor. He didn't like the way Marissa constantly pushed Nina beyond the realm of common sense. A few years earlier, Nina and Marissa had gotten drunk on Buttershots and came knocking at Connor's window in the middle of the night. Connor had opened the window reluctantly, and Marissa demanded he let them in to see Sam's room. Connor could tell it was Marissa's idea by the way Nina wouldn't meet his gaze; when he said "no", Marissa told him to stop being such a dickhead about it. He immediately slammed the window shut and hadn't really spoken to her ever since. Rumor had it she was perilously close to not graduating on time and was taking every extra assignment she could get her hands on in hopes of squeaking over the finish line. Hence, she had no time for lunch in the cafeteria.

The entire table stared at Connor in mild surprise, and a sly smile crept across Nina's lips, as if it was exactly what she'd been expecting to happen. "And how may we help you today, Quikstuff?" she said.

"Heatseeker," Connor replied. "I need you to tell me what you know."

Nina winced. "Rough trade right there, my friend. That info is for discerning ears only."

Connor's face flushed, slightly angered. He should have expected she'd do some dumb song and dance in front of her friends. "And how come you get to decide whose ears are discerning?"

She smiled. "Because I've actually heard them."

Connor didn't buy it for a second. "No way. I've been searching for years. If there was anything out there I would have found it by now."

Nina shook her head. "Which is exactly why you haven't. They aren't online; you can't just 'find' them. That's the point. That's not what they're about. That's not what their music is about. You have to earn it. That's why they're special. And the fact that you don't realize it is all the proof I need that you emphatically do not get it. Now move along, please. You're tainting the remainder of my high school cafeteria experience."

Nina turned toward Faraz in an attempt to ignore Connor, but he didn't budge. "So how did you get it, Nina?" he asked. "How did you earn it?"

"I went looking. Same way you did. But I was obviously much smarter about it. And I didn't stop. I never stopped."

Faraz snickered. "That, and you sent a picture of your bare feet to some rando on Reddit in exchange for an MP3 that may or may not actually be the band."

Nina threw up her hands. "Seriously, Fuzz?" Nina was the only one who called him that. She had a serious thing for nicknames.

Faraz smirked. "You know I can't stand idly by and watch you high-road it when I know for a fact that you're actively full of crap. It's basically a defining characteristic of my personality."

Connor sensed his opening. "Let me hear the song and I'll never bother you again."

"Nice try," Nina said. "Four more periods then you'll never bother me again anyway."

"Seriously, Nina."

"It's on my phone. And I promised the guy—"

"I believe his username was *kingofnopants*." Faraz couldn't help himself.

"Thank you for that, Fuzz. I promised the king I wouldn't send it to anyone. So I can't."

It was so close, Connor could taste it. "So let me borrow your phone then. Five minutes. Then I'll bring it right back, and I'm a ghost. I've never once asked you for anything. And I never will again."

It was the truth, and Nina knew it.

Her heartstrings sufficiently tugged, she whipped her phone out and cued up the song. She handed it over to Connor as she locked eyes with him. "You have no idea what you're about to hear. This band will forever change your pathetic existence. This band will save your life."

-

Connor took Nina's phone out to the quad and found a shady spot on the lawn as far away from everyone else as possible. He stared at the triangular play button on the screen as it beckoned to him. It was a weirdly tense moment…all the years of wondering were about to come to an end.

He reached back and tried to pull up some notion of what he thought Heatseeker would sound like, but he honestly had no idea. He drew a supermassive black-hole blank. Sam had listened to a lot of loud, angry, yell-y music in the last era of their time together, but Connor couldn't really tell one band from the next. There was only so much angst a pre-teen could handle before his circuitry overloaded. But none of that mattered anymore, and now it was time to find out.

Connor took a deep breath and pressed play.

An immediate squeal of vicious feedback made him reflexively reach up to pull the earbuds out until he realized it was intentional. Then the guitar started. It was distant and haunting, like it was floating in from another room somewhere.

Before the song fully kicked in, Nina's phone chirped with a text from Marissa: *Frag Dave just texted. Charity case stopped by the table? WTF?!? Sux enough you have to sacrifice 15 mins of your morning every day because your mom is worried he'll off himself once he finally realizes no one cares about him.*

Marissa's words punched right through his gut. Connor ripped the earbuds out and started marching back toward the cafeteria before he was even fully aware he was doing it. He could feel large, stinging tears building up behind his eyes and knew he only had a few seconds until they would force their way through.

Nina's brow pinched in confusion as she watched him approach. It was obvious that something was wrong, but Connor was way past caring. He flipped her phone aggressively in the vicinity of the table as he stormed by.

Nina lunged for it. "What the hell?"

But Connor didn't stop.

He walked out of the cafeteria, back through the hall, past his locker, out through the front doors and into the sunlight.

His high school career was officially done.

4

Connor could remember that when he was younger, his Dad had told him the best walks usually happened when you didn't have anywhere specific to go. His logic was this: if you're walking somewhere in particular, chances are you're already there in your mind. Which means you're already thinking about what you have to do once you get there, how much time you have to do it, and where you have to go afterward. There isn't space for anything else. But if all you're doing is thinking, and the physical act of walking is secondary, you can go just about anywhere in your mind and eventually you'll look up and realize you're somewhere that you maybe never had any intention of going in the first place.

It was the difference between an adventure and an errand.

And that was how Connor ended up standing in front of Finer Foods Grocery on Lake Street.

He had walked straight out of Westerberg High four periods too early, chock full of righteous indignation that gave way to embarrassment and hurt feelings in the span of three blocks. He spent the next hour crafting all the perfect insults he would never actually have the balls to say to Marissa in a hundred years, whenever the fictitious showdown between the two of them would take place.

But eventually he started to think about whether anyone actually cared about him at all. Was his mom cognizant enough to know when he was in the house? And even if she was, did it matter to her? Her broken psyche certainly appeared to offer up a resounding "no".

The things that hurt the most to hear are typically that way because, on some level, at least part of them are true. And somewhere around minute twenty-five of Connor's walk, he realized that was the case. What Marissa had texted was flippant and bitchy, but it also felt true.

As Connor stared up at the Finer Foods sign, it hit him that he had no idea how long he'd been standing there. He figured he should probably go inside and buy something.

He didn't have a lot of money, and he wasn't especially hungry, so he roamed the aisles aimlessly for a few minutes, waiting for some type of impulse or desire to present itself. The bakery counter had a bunch of extra staff working, slammed with orders for some slight variation of the exact same "Congratulations Graduate!" cake for all the other kids in his class. Maybe that was what he should do: get himself a congratulatory present. Not a cake, necessarily…but something he would never get under ordinary circumstances.

He headed toward the baking supplies, guided toward something in particular, more by instinct than conscious thought. He couldn't remember seeing them the last few times he'd been there. But he turned the corner, and there they were, clipped onto a cheap cardboard display hanging off the shelf next to the boxes of Krusteaz pancake and waffle mix. He and Dad had always joked about buying one, and now he finally would. It would be his tribute.

Connor plucked the stainless-steel Tyrannosaurus Rex pancake form off the display hook and made his way toward the self-check, the only graduation present he'd ever receive firmly in tow.

Connor was excellent when it came to making pancakes. The key was to use a teaspoon of vegetable oil and a teaspoon of butter in the skillet for every pancake, to crisp the edges. He wished he could make some for Dad. Or anyone, really. Even if just so someone else could confirm how good they were.

But the number one disappointing thing about dinosaur-shaped pancakes was that they tasted exactly like regular-shaped pancakes.

He washed and dried and put away the dishes, then grabbed his book bag off the counter and headed for his room to unpack all his school stuff for the very last time.

The stupid yearbook was in there.

It was a conduit back to that afternoon, which now felt even worse somehow.

He opened it up and was greeted by the crack of the fresh spine. The pages were glossy, and he flipped softly through a few. He'd always wondered why some of the pictures were black and white while others were color…was it a cost thing? A style choice? And who got to decide? Was that the real reason they had a yearbook club in the first place? If it were up to him, they would all be black and white. Pictures were just shadows, anyway—things that already happened and would never happen the same way again.

He scanned everyone's faces. Their smiles and their eyes and best-friends-forever-with-arms-around-each-other poses and their biggest, brightest memories. None of it meant anything to him.

He stopped at a picture of Nina and Marissa. Marissa had her tongue out, pretending she didn't want her picture taken while posing deliberately at the same time. But all Connor cared about was the Heatseeker patch on Nina's coat.

He checked his watch. School was out…she should have gotten home by now. He strode out of his room and took the yearbook with him.

Nina answered sometime during Connor's third set of knocks. She gave him her very best drop-dead glare as he held up the yearbook. "Would you sign this for me?" he asked. "You can make it out to 'Charity Case'."

Nina grabbed the yearbook and flipped through all the empty signature pages. "Gee, Connor. I wonder why someone would ever think of you like that. What's the point of even getting a yearbook?"

Connor snatched it back. "It was Chase Heffernan's. I inherited it because he told Danielle Gutter to do something very specific and disgusting to herself. And why would I want anyone to sign it? So I can get the same recycled 'sorry about your dad and your brother' message over and over. I'm sick of everyone feeling sorry for me all the time."

Nina shook her head. "Okay, dude. Real talk. You're sick of that?"

Connor nodded.

She lit into him. "You wanna know why everyone only thinks of you as the kid who lost his dad and his brother? Why everyone feels bad for you all the time? Because that's all you are to them. You're nothing else. You talk to no one. You interact with no one. You don't do anything. What else are you supposed to be? How else are they supposed to see you? What do you do all day when we aren't in school, Connor? What makes you happy—sitting around your house, hoping your dad and your brother will magically walk through the front door?"

Connor was shaken. "That's not fair."

Nina got in his face. "You're goddamn right it's not. But it's reality; it's what happened. And nothing you can do will change that. If Sam and your dad really are still out there somewhere, it would break their hearts to think of you like this. You've gotta move on with your life, Connor. You've gotta do something."

Connor wiped at his eyes with his sleeve. "Take me to the show tonight, then. Let's start there. I need to see Heatseeker. I need to be there. That's something."

Nina rolled her eyes. "Seriously…"

"Don't give me that, 'you have to earn it' crap again. You never would have heard of them if it wasn't for Sam. You know it. So you owe him for that. And since he isn't here at the moment, I'll serve as proxy."

Nina softened. "You know he's not gonna be there tonight, right Connor? I mean, you have to know that."

Connor shrugged. "No. I have to believe he will. Otherwise, what's the point of any of it?"

Nina caved. "They're playing at The Black Hole. It's way out on Thatcher, right before McCaughan Woods. Faraz is bugging out because he's already driving six of us and his dad's jeep only seats five. So you'll have to figure out your own way."

Connor nodded. "Can you text me directions?"

Nina whipped her phone out. "What's your number?"

Connor half smiled. "Hilarious."

Nina glared at him. "I'm serious."

Connor shook his head. "You don't have my number?"

Nina shrugged. "Why would I?"

Connor couldn't help but be stung. "I don't know. We've only lived next door to each other for the last fourteen years."

Nina handed him her phone for the second time that day. "That's not really a reason. Here. Put it in. And just so you know, The Black Hole is legit. It's divey and dark and smells like piss. And some of the regulars aren't so stoked about first-timers, so maybe try a little harder not to dress like such an undercover Boy Scout."

Connor handed her phone back. "Yeah. Thanks."

She smiled. "You have no idea what you're in for tonight."

-

Connor rifled through Sam's closet, worried about what he was going to wear for the first time in his entire teenage existence. He searched through Sam's old band t-shirts, which were all a slight variation of the exact same thing: black fabric with the band name written across the top in aggressive handwriting, with a washed-out logo underneath. None of the specific names meant anything to him. He was worried that somehow he'd end up picking the wrong one. So he took an alternate approach and pulled down Sam's all-time favorite thrift store score. It was a Kelly-green t-shirt with a cartoon drawing of an Italian chef holding up a pizza in celebration, with the words *Green Lantern Pizza & Tavern* printed across the chest in big white letters. Sam said Green Lantern used to be a biker hangout on the edge of town that closed in the mid-'80s after one of their employees tried to break up a fist fight in the parking lot and was stabbed in the head for his trouble. So the shirt was a legitimate find.

It felt like the right choice for his first show.

His first show.

He almost couldn't believe it. His first time ever seeing a real band. He and Sam almost tagged along with Mom and Dad once out of necessity when they went to see Tom Petty at The White River Amphitheater in Auburn, but Mrs. Slade from their church came through at the last minute and said she'd babysit. He'd always figured Sam would take him to his first real concert one day. That definitely felt like it was supposed to be a big brother/little brother rite of passage. And one of the most important ones.

As he tossed the t-shirt over his shoulder, his eyes settled on Sam's drawing on the wall. The framed action shot of the band mid-song that was Connor's all-time favorite.

He lifted it off the wall and took it with him, frame and all.

5

Connor's chest heaved as his lungs burned through the warm summer air. It had been way too long since he'd ridden a bike. So long, in fact, that it had taken him forty-five minutes to dig it out of the back of the garage, lubricate the chain, check the brake lines, adjust the seat and fill the tires with air. And he didn't know how to do any of those things, so most of that time was actively spent watching tutorials on YouTube.

In the brief span it had taken Connor to get from the end of his driveway to cutting across the little league field in Goldsmith Park, he'd decided that riding a bike in the summer was one of the great undeniable pleasures in life. It would be his go-to mode of transportation now whenever the weather was nice enough. He should probably invest in a better bike, he thought. Maybe he could even become a bike guy—like that could be his thing. He'd never really had a *thing* before, other than being the kid with the missing dad and brother. Maybe Nina was right. High school was over now; maybe he didn't have to be that kid anymore. Not if he didn't want to.

He couldn't remember specifically, but he was sure Evergreen had at least one bike shop. He should check to see if they were hiring. Working at a bike shop might actually be cool, and he'd already taught himself the basics on YouTube.

Connor felt hot streaks of sweat seeping through Sam's t-shirt beneath the straps of his backpack and all down his back. He couldn't find a lock in the garage, which meant he'd have to leave the bike somewhere in McCaughan Woods once he got to The Black Hole, so the only things in the pack were Sam's framed drawing and a hoodie for the ride back in case it cooled off later. As far as Connor was concerned, the drawing was a million times more important than the bike anyway.

He never even saw the patch of loose gravel in the parking lot at the west end of the park.

The back tire skidded out from under him as the entire rear of the bike swung wildly to the left. Connor made a sloppy, frantic over-correction attempting to regain control, but he still ended up sprawled out on his back on the ground with a fresh rip in his jeans and a trickle of blood seeping from his knee. He laid there for a few moments, marinating in his own embarrassment before he looked up at the sky and noticed the sun beginning to set.

It was nearly dark by the time Connor stashed the bike in McCaughan Woods. He hid it next to a row of gigantic spruce trees, a few hundred feet up the old, slightly paved access road that ran behind The Black Hole.

Suddenly, he was there.

He had actually made it.

The bar looked like an oversized log cabin that had been built very quickly and angrily by someone with a deep-seated hatred for log cabins. The logs were all rough and unsanded and came in a wide variety of shades and sizes. Most of them jutted out of the walls well past where they should have stopped, and all of them were carved into sharp, splintered points at the top. The overall effect was overt and aggressive, as if the building itself was saying, "Don't even think about it."

A wave of anxiety doused Connor's nerves as he cut around the side of the building. The small dirt parking lot was so full of cars that people had started parking on the lawn around it. There was already a long line formed out front.

He recognized Faraz's dad's jeep in the grass, but he didn't see Nina or any of her reject lunch table compatriots anywhere in line. *They must already be inside,* he thought. At least he would know someone there. He hoped she'd let him stand near them, even though there was a distinct possibility none of them would acknowledge him anyway. That was fine. As long as he didn't have to talk to Marissa.

Connor headed to the back of the line. He felt every set of eyes judge him as he passed. They stared right through him once they'd determined he wasn't someone they'd recognized or anyone cool enough to care about.

He got in line behind a guy and a girl who looked like they were a few years older than him. They had matching fire-engine red hair; he could tell their dye jobs were fresh by the bright-red stains on their palms. They regarded Connor for a moment as they passed their vape pen back and forth. Fire-Hair Guy nodded toward Connor's knee. "Cool blood."

Connor glanced down at his ripped jeans and skinned knee.

Fire-Hair Girl gave him a weird look. "What's with the backpack? You some kind of Boy Scout?"

Connor shook his head and laughed. "I brought something for the band. It's the only way I could carry it."

Fire-Hair Guy nodded. "They probably won't let you bring it in. Not that it matters anyway."

Connor gripped the straps of the pack defensively. "What do you mean?"

Fire-Hair Girl took another long pull from the pen. "Sold out, man. Max capacity. This is the reject line. If anyone leaves, then we get in. Fat chance, though. I believe you're number seventy-nine. So only seventy-eight superfans have to skedaddle in order for you to get into Wonderland."

Fire-Hair Guy raised his red stained hand. "Seventy-eight. Nice to meet you."

Connor shook his head. "But it's basically the only thing that matters in my whole life right now. I have to get in there."

Fire-Hair Girl yawned. "So do we all, man. Go plead your case, though. Tell them something they haven't already heard seventy-eight times. Maybe they'll take pity on you."

Connor took an antsy step to the side and scanned the line all the way up to the front. There was a mountain of a man just outside the door, an enormous, morbidly-obese bouncer, firmly planted on top of a buckling stool that was holding on for dear life. He locked eyes with Connor. It took Connor an entire half-second to determine that there was no possible way he was going to get in. But he had to try anyway.

He casually crept toward the front of the line. Once he was halfway up, most of the other kids that were stuck waiting realized what he was going to do and booed him loudly. Connor was undeterred. He started up the steps toward the bouncer, who was grinning right at him. He didn't even wait for Connor's attempt before he sneered, "Don't even think about it."

Connor opened his mouth, then thought better of it and scampered away. All the kids at the front of the line applauded mockingly.

He snuck around the side of the building, hoping if he moved quick enough he'd somehow leave all his disappointment at the front of the line. But as he plopped down in the grass and leaned back against the building he felt the sting of failure cover him like an itchy blanket.

A squeal of rusty hinges pulled him out of it.

He stood up and clocked a beat-to-crap cargo van on the edge of the parking lot. The split rear doors were wide open, and someone was digging around inside.

Connor hustled up to the van and let loose an insecure "Excuse me?" An older man popped his head out and stared Connor down. He looked cool, rock-and-roll and spectacularly weathered, like some ancient biker who'd been out riding in the hard desert sun for far too long. Connor caught a quick flash of the guy's belt, a laminated badge with the same Heatseeker H-and-S shield logo that was currently hanging over Sam's bed.

Connor started in. "Are you with Heatseeker? I'm hoping you are, because of the van and the pass on your belt. I know the logo… it's on a poster in my brother's room. He made it himself."

Cool Old Biker said nothing.

Connor shifted nervously. "My brother saw Heatseeker a long time ago. They were all he ever talked about afterward. Five years ago, he and my dad went missing, and I haven't seen him since. I'm hoping he might be inside for the show, which I know sounds pretty dumb. But at the very least, I was hoping I could see the band. That way Sam and I would be connected again. For a little bit, at least."

If any of this meant anything to Cool Old Biker, he definitely didn't show it.

Connor reached down and started unzipping the backpack, sensing it was last resort time. "I brought one of Sam's drawings with me. It's of the band. And it's really good. Probably my favorite drawing of his ever, actually. I was hoping to show it to them." The man turned back around and continued rifling through the van. Connor's heart dropped, but he finished pulling the framed drawing out anyway. "Could you take a look? Just for a second? I think it will…I don't know, I guess prove to you what a big fan he was or something? I'm just asking you for a break, man. The world hasn't given me a single break in the last five years. Not one. And I know it's not fair for me to ask you for one but—"

Cool Old Biker ripped the drawing and the backpack from Connor's grasp and tossed them in the back of the van.

Before Connor could register what had happened enough to be pissed off, Cool Old Biker heaved a guitar amp into Connor's arms, slammed the van doors shut, and headed back toward The Black Hole. He circled around to the back of the building as Connor scrambled to keep up, following deliberately with the heavy amp cradled in his arms.

Connor rounded the side and saw a different entrance and a different bouncer. This one was a skinny kid with a stripe of green hair and his face buried in his phone. The man held up his pass. Green Hair Bouncer barely even looked up as he nodded.

Cool Old Biker motioned for Connor to follow him in. Connor took a quick look around, waiting for someone to spring out and stop him. There was no way in Hell this was actually going to work. But no one was coming.

He took in a big breath of fresh forest air, then disappeared inside The Black Hole.

He walked into a tiny room with an old couch losing its stuffing in the corner, stacked cases of bottled water that stretched practically up to ceiling, and a table full of instrument cables, all neatly wrapped, taped and sorted. Cool Old Biker nodded at the amp in Connor's arms, then pointed at the ground between the table and the tower of bottled water.

As Connor set the amp down, he peeked across the room toward a slightly open door. There was a handwritten note taped to the front that read simply: Heatseeker. He could hear people talking softly inside, and he knew they were in there. He drifted slowly toward the room without even realizing it.

But Cool Old Biker put his palm on Connor's chest and stopped him dead in his tracks. He pointed in the opposite direction, toward a hallway across the room.

Connor reached out to shake the man's hand, but it never appeared.

So he headed for the hallway instead.

-

The longer Connor walked the hallway, the darker it got. Finally, a small sliver of light bled through the gap between the door and the frame, and he inched his way toward it. He reached out blindly until his fingers found the cool, hard wood of the door. He pressed his ear up against it and listened. There was music on the other side, and the murmur of a hundred different voices talking at once.

He took a moment to absorb it all as he stood in the dark, completely alone, before he opened the door slowly and walked out into the light.

He assumed it would be industrial, with lots of black iron and concrete—that somehow, every surface would be dripping wet, and there would be chains hanging from the ceiling and a bunch of maniacs revving chainsaws and spitting fire. A real *Fury Road* motif. But the inside of The Black Hole kind of reminded him of his Uncle Walter's basement. It had wood paneled walls, a bunch of hokey, vintage neon beer signs and a shuffleboard table over by the front door. The obvious highlight was a giant moose head mounted above the bar that wore a pair of oversized novelty sunglasses and a Cowboy's Butts Drive Me Nuts trucker hat.

A mass of bodies pushed back and forth in front of him, fighting to work their way up to the front of the bar, then fighting to get back to whatever spot they'd originated from. The stage was on the other side of the room, directly across from the bar, and was probably a few seconds away from collapsing. It looked like it was just a mass of plywood and garage sale tables nailed together, with some ancient carpeting stapled on top for good measure.

At each corner there was a nearly beaten-to-death PA speaker aimed out toward the crowd. A mic with neon blue tape on the bottom sat waiting in its stand in the middle of the stage. The drums were set up right behind that, with the Heatseeker 'H' and 'S' shield logo that Connor had stared at every day for years printed on the front head of the kick drum. The bass rig was to the right of the drums, with a large white lightning bolt spray-painted on the mesh front of the speaker. Connor knew just enough to recognize that the guitar cabinet was an Orange, which was apparently really good; Sam had said he wanted to save up and get one once he and Dad finished the Hagstrom.

Connor watched as Cool Old Biker climbed up onstage carrying the amp he'd brought in. He was amazed that no one really paid much attention. It was like anyone could have just walked right up onstage if they'd wanted to…not that *he* ever would have. Not in a million years.

The man set the amp on top of the Orange speaker and unrolled two cables, then plugged one into the front and one into the back. He guided the front cable neatly through the handle on top of the amp, then flicked it on. The amp's red power light awakened and glowed brightly, signaling to all that it was armed and ready. Then Cool Old Biker hopped down off the stage and quickly disappeared back down the hallway, which Connor figured meant the band would be coming out soon. He scanned the crowd.

He knew in an instant that Sam wasn't there.

He had felt it in his gut the second he stepped into the main room, but he held out a momentary sliver of hope anyway. It had been five years since Connor had seen him, so Sam could have looked completely different. But he knew there was no possible way he wouldn't recognize his brother immediately.

He looked back and forth across the entire crowd twice and by the end of his second pass he felt the hope fade away. A part of him was relieved. He didn't want to imagine Sam being back in town and not coming to see him right away.

Connor noticed Bailey, though. He was six-four, which made him and his weirdo goth hair super easy to spot. He was with Nina and the rest of their crew off to the right of the stage, practically at the front. Connor considered staying by himself in the back, but he hadn't ridden his bike all this way and snuck into the show just to stand there alone. So he worked his way toward them, one squeeze-through and sheepish apology at a time.

Marissa spotted him first and rolled her eyes so hard her head couldn't help but follow. But he could've sworn Nina was holding back a surprised grin as she watched him walk up. He shoved his way in, and her group reluctantly spread open, just wide enough for him to sneak his shoulder between Fragile Dave and Faraz. Everyone stared at each other for a full minute with no clear idea what to say. Connor's presence had obviously thrown off the group's equilibrium.

Then, for some reason unbeknownst even to him, Connor decided to take the plunge and yelled out over the noise. "I can't believe I actually got in. I rode my bike here, and there's a huge line of rejects out front, and these kids said I would never get in, and then I went up to talk to the bouncer and he was like, 'No way!', but there's this guy who works for the band and—"

Marissa yelled over him. "Faraz, what time is your dad leaving for Bellingham tomorrow?"

Faraz glanced at Connor, fully aware of what Marissa was trying to do. "Three o'clock. I already told you that."

Marissa eyed Connor coldly. "So what time should we come over to start setting up for the party?"

Faraz shifted uncomfortably. "Whenever."

Marissa smiled. "We're having a party at Faraz's dad's house tomorrow, Connor. We would invite you to come, but…you know. No."

Connor shrugged. "Don't sweat it. I'm not a charity case."

Marissa's cheeks flushed, and Nina definitely cracked a smile this time. "Marissa, don't be such a hag," she said. "Connor, I'm sure Faraz wouldn't care if you wanted to come by."

Faraz's head bobbed lightly in time to the beat of the background music. "Whatever, man. Just bring a swimsuit if you wanna go in the hot tub. Also, don't take a dump in the hot tub. One time, Jason Vokler came over and demolished an entire bag of burgers from Dick's and then turbochugged like four Rainiers in twenty minutes and got a little too comfortable in there, and the next thing I know the circulation pump is all jacked up and my dad made me buy a new one. They're like a hundred and fifty bucks. It sucked."

Connor nodded hesitantly. "Um, sure. No problem."

The lights dimmed, the background music abruptly cut out and everyone whipped around and stared at the stage. It was intensely silent until some dickhead yelled out "Whooo!"

Then suddenly, they were there.

They cut a swath through the crowd and climbed onstage. They looked exactly like Connor had always thought they would.

Like they'd just walked right out of Sam's drawing.

The bass player held her black Gibson Ripper low at her right hip, then lifted it up and twisted it out in front of her. She plugged it in, and her amp buzzed loudly. The sides of her head were shaved, and her long, crimson mohawk hung softly in front of her face, slightly obscuring her electric-blue eyes ringed with wide streaks of thick black eyeshadow. Connor noticed she had the Heatseeker shield logo tattooed high up on her right arm; it peeked out from under where the sleeve had been torn off her t-shirt. She turned and glared out at the crowd, daring anyone to meet her gaze.

The drummer took a seat behind his kit. He was a stark contrast to the bassist, with sandy chin-length hair tucked behind his ears, held in place by a red-white-and-blue headband, a half-buttoned short-sleeve flannel shirt, and a wholesome, aww-shucks face that was lightly covered by a few days' worth of peach fuzz. He also had the shield logo tattooed on his right arm, but his was on the inside of his wrist. He blasted a few beats on his kick drum and rolled rapidly on his snare. Connor felt every hit deep in his stomach. The drummer stopped abruptly, then twirled his sticks in the air, ready to go.

The singer unzipped his hoodie and wrapped it neatly around the base of the mic stand. He looked like he was a few years younger than the bassist and the drummer. He was lanky and rail thin, with black frame glasses and his hair buzzed close on the sides but longer on his crown, like a good old-fashioned military flat top. Connor didn't think he'd ever actually seen anyone close to his age with that kind of haircut before. He wore a two-sizes-too-small Wienerschnitzel ringer t-shirt, and as he reached up to tap the mic and check it, Connor noticed the shield logo tattooed on the inside of his bicep.

The guitar player strode on stage last, gripping his Telecaster by the neck. He appeared to be the oldest of the four and looked like a classic rock-and-roll throwback, with long curls of golden hair, well-worn jeans and a 3/4 sleeve white and navy baseball shirt. He plugged into his amp and tuned his guitar. He looked perfectly and effortlessly cool, as if he were destined to be on stage holding a guitar since the moment he was born. He finished tuning, then looked up and locked eyes with the rest of the band.

The singer leaned into the mic. "You know who we are and why you're here." He took a quick step back, dropped his head and swayed slowly in place.

The guitar started quietly at first, playing a twinkling, repetitive melody that was soft and haunting. Connor felt all the tiny hairs on his arms stand on end. The guitar player strummed faster and harder, the initial melody faded as the intensity built, and then the rest of the band jumped in.

The entire room exploded.

Connor was shoved forward as everyone behind him surged toward the stage like a tidal wave. The music was faster and louder than anything he'd ever heard before. It was beautiful and guttural and made him feel like a part of his heart he never knew existed had just come to life and was on fire.

A smile broke across his lips and he hurled himself against the massive sea of moving bodies. All his thoughts of being alone, all his nightmares, all his doubts and worries disappeared in a lightning flash of fuzzed-out bliss and pure volume. For the first time in a very long time, Connor was allowed to just feel like a kid and enjoy all the weightlessness that provided.

And as the first song ended, he realized nothing would ever be the same again.

6

The rest of the show was a frenetic blur that felt like it went by in seconds. Before he knew it, Connor was outside in the grass next to the parking lot, surrounded by Nina and her crew and buzzing from a massive jolt of energy like he'd never felt before. He wanted to sprint a thousand miles straight up a mountain in the middle of the pouring rain to fist-fight a grizzly bear while screaming Heatseeker songs the entire way.

A cool, heavy breeze crept out of the woods, and suddenly Connor realized that Sam's shirt was drenched all the through with sweat. He peeled it away from his stomach, and it released with a wet smack. He looked up and locked eyes with Nina. They had a bond now. A genuine moment that connected them forever. Maybe this would finally help turn them into friends after all these years.

Faraz talked rapidly between gulps of damp air while he worked to catch his breath. "Connor, man. We're going for pancakes at

Cozy Corner. Wanna come? We can squeeze you into the jeep somewhere."

Before Connor had the chance to corroborate his shiny new plans, there was a sudden burst of activity, and a crowd formed back toward The Black Hole. Connor broke from Nina and the others and snuck through just in time to see the band shove the last of their equipment into the back of their beat-up cargo van and disappear inside.

Cool Old Biker slammed the back doors closed, then turned and gave the crowd a cursory salute before he hopped into the driver's seat. A line of bouncers streamed into the lot and formed a row in front of the old, slightly paved access road that ran up into the woods behind The Black Hole.

The cargo van roared to life, lurched forward, and belched out a thick black cloud of exhaust. The bouncers slid apart as the van inched passed them, then quickly fell back in line once it went by, forming a human barricade that prevented anyone from attempting to follow.

The van sped up and rocked back and forth on the uneven gravel before it eventually found its footing and took off. Connor watched the ember-glow of the taillights as they disappeared from sight.

The crowd dissipated quickly, bummed by the hasty departure of their heroes. Connor turned and walked directly into Faraz. He had no idea he was standing right behind him. Faraz looked extra disappointed for some reason. "Why'd they take off so fast? And what's the deal with driving into the woods? There's literally nothing back there but more woods."

Connor noticed Faraz's homemade shirt for the first time. It had Heatseeker written across the chest, only the Seeker had a line through it. Underneath, it was rewritten, but this time it was spelled Seaker; this was crossed out also. Then underneath that it was written a third time and read Seeker once again. Connor stared at Faraz quizzically. Faraz shook his head. "I don't know what I'm supposed to wear to a rock show, so I figured I'd just make my own shirt. Marissa was the first one over, and she swore that I spelled it wrong. I know how to spell the word, but she insisted that the band spelled it differently and told me I'd look ridiculous. I don't get why anybody thinks it's cool to spell things wrong intentionally, but whatever. So I believed her. Nina came in five minutes later and told me what was up. I swear, I never knew a girl could be a dick until I met Marissa."

Connor liked Faraz more by the second.

Nina and everyone else appeared. She stood on her tiptoes and gazed down the access road. "So that was super weird."

Faraz shook his head, dejected. As Connor stared at his homemade shirt, it hit him: Sam's drawing and his book bag were still in Heatseeker's van. His head dropped. "So stupid…"

Faraz scoffed, mock-offended. "The shirt isn't that bad."

But Connor was already sprinting for his bike.

Faraz yelled after him, "Dude! Where are you going?"

Connor was twenty steps past the bouncers by the time they noticed him, but it didn't matter anyway. The band was long gone by now. He fished his bike out from behind the row of spruce trees and pedaled off into the night.

-

Ten minutes into his trip, Connor realized that riding his bike with no headlight in the middle of the woods late at night while under the cover of hundred-and-fifty-foot-tall spruce trees had to be the darkest situation he'd ever been in in his life. Sure, it wasn't lost-in-a-cave dark, or Mariana Trench dark, but it was easily the darkest thing a normal kid who'd grown up under the normal stars and normal streetlights in a normal town had ever encountered.

Connor pedaled silently and slowly, convinced that any second now his front tire would catch the big rock that would flip his bike and leave him paralyzed. He wanted to give up and turn back, but he knew deep down that he couldn't. He had to get Sam's drawing back.

So he tried to focus on his breathing to calm down and distract himself from the hundreds of malicious rocks he was positive were lying in wait. Then, for the second time that night, he crashed his bike. This time it really wasn't his fault though; there was no possible way he could've seen the van parked in the middle of the road with its lights turned off.

Connor squirmed up off the ground, triumphantly unparalyzed, and limped slowly toward the van. He assumed there was no one inside; he'd just slammed directly into it and had yet to witness a response. But he knocked swiftly on the side door anyway, just in case.

After a few seconds of heavy silence, he walked around to the driver's side, cupped his hands around his eyes to peer in the window, realized how ridiculous that was, and then just tried the door. It was unlocked. As Connor opened it, the sudden, devastating brightness from the overhead interior light forced him to step back instinctively and shield his eyes.

His gaze dropped, and he tracked a considerably larger stream of blood through the tear in the front of his jeans now. He shivered as he watched big, fat droplets slowly work their way down his shin. He gripped inside the door frame, stepped up on to the side panel with his good leg, and peered into the van. It was empty...and something about the entire situation suddenly and very thoroughly creeped him the hell out.

He scanned the panel in the door for the unlock switch, pressed it seventeen times in ten seconds for good measure, then scurried around to the back of the van. All he wanted was to find Sam's drawing and his book bag as quickly as possible so he could get to the next awesome part of his trip, the one where he had to speed-ride home through the pitch black forest totally alone.

As his hand closed around the cold steel of the door handle, a deep, angry growl echoed from somewhere deep in the woods. The noise surrounded him, as if it was coming from every direction at once somehow.

Connor felt his spine turn to ice.

He stumbled away from the van while his eyes scanned frantically through the dark. He backed straight off the access road, back into the woods, and before he'd even decided to do it, he was sprinting away from the van, further into the trees. He knew it was the wrong thing to do; he screamed his head off routinely every time some dumb teenage camp counselor did it in one of the slasher movies he and Sam used to watch. But he couldn't help it. He was terrified beyond the capacity for rational thought.

There was a fresh crack of heavy branches to his left, and he sped up. Something was getting close. Every sensory receptor in his body screamed it at him. Heat built up in his legs, and he felt his shin tingle where he was cut. It was itchy, and he wondered if it was weird to think about being itchy while he was running for his life.

He slammed into something very hard at full speed, and ended up sprawled on his back. He felt ridiculous a few seconds later once he realized his feet were moving, as if he were still trying to run.

A pair of strong hands grabbed his forearm and yanked him up. Connor staggered back, drunk on adrenaline and fear. "You okay, kid?" It was a man's voice, soft and genuinely concerned.

Connor stared right into the face of Heatseeker's guitarist, Mr. Effortlessly Cool. The Golden Boy. He reached toward Connor slowly, trying not to spook him, which would have been impossible because Connor was completely entranced. "Heatseeker," he whispered softly.

Golden Boy grasped Connor's arm and held him steady. "You shouldn't be out here."

A hungry roar bellowed out in the dark, somewhere closer.

Golden Boy instinctively stepped in front of Connor. "I'm about to ask you a pretty big question. But don't be afraid. Just tell me the truth and everything will be alright. Cool?"

Connor nodded, but it felt like nothing would ever be cool or alright again. Knots of dread bubbled up in his stomach, and his eyes drifted off. There was something in the distance…and whatever it was would come crashing through the trees any second now. He had never been so sure of anything.

Golden Boy grabbed Connor by the shoulders and forced him to meet his gaze. He leaned in close, and without a hint of trepidation in his voice asked, "Do you want to die?"

The answer slipped through Connor's lips and hung softly in the air. "No." Connor surprised himself with how quickly he answered, given that most days he typically didn't feel like there was a whole lot left to live for.

Golden Boy smiled. "That's what I was hoping you'd say."

He gently cradled Connor's face in his hands. There was a warmth in his touch; Connor felt it build in his temples and spread slowly down through his shoulders, along his spine, into his stomach, and down his legs, until eventually all the fear and tension in his body released and dissipated completely.

He looked up in awe, but Golden Boy's expression was vacant and blank as his eyelids flittered open and closed. His head snapped down quickly, and suddenly he was back. He smiled at Connor with an ease and a sense of familiarity, as if he had known him his entire life. "There. That wasn't so bad, w—" Golden Boy was ripped into the air violently as something enormous sank its fangs into the meat of his shoulder.

Connor backed away from the jet-black mass of fur as it lifted the guitarist higher and higher in its massive jaws. Whatever it was, it had be at least 8 feet tall.

Connor locked eyes with Golden Boy. He had no idea what he was supposed to do now, and he was heartbroken for whatever part he had played in bringing them to this moment. But there was no fear or anger in the guitarist's face. Only warmth. And acceptance. As if he'd always known this was exactly what was supposed to happen.

The muscle and tissue in Golden Boy's shoulder finally gave. He slid out of the creature's bloody mouth and dropped down to the forest floor with a wet *thud*.

The creature let out a deafening roar, then lowered its head and continued feeding. Its claws ripped away long strands of skin. Connor figured he only had a few seconds left before it finished Golden Boy off for good, then turned its attention toward him. It felt perfectly fitting somehow that he was going to die now, just moments after realizing how much he wanted to live.

A tiny spark of red fire hissed through the trees and struck the creature dead-center in its back. The creature's head twisted, and it bellowed loudly in pain and fury. Then its gaze locked on Connor.

Connor closed his eyes and waited for razor teeth to rip into his skin and tear him apart, but it never came. The rest of Heatseeker—plus Cool Old Biker—exploded out of the woods at full speed.

The bass player was in the lead, wielding some sort of homemade spear. "Topper!" she screamed as she drove it toward the creature's side. But the creature turned away, brought its front leg down swiftly, and splintered the spear in half.

The creature growled furiously, eyeing Connor and the band as it weighed its odds. There was not a doubt in Connor's mind it could take them all out right then if it wanted to. But it dropped back slowly, never breaking its gaze, until it was swallowed up by the cover of the woods.

The drummer rushed over to what was left of the guitar player scattered on the ground. The bass player stared at Connor and marched toward him angrily. "What did you do?"

The drummer slid his arms under Golden Boy and was instantly covered in his blood. "Doesn't matter right now, Sarah," he said. "Get over here. I need you."

-

Connor ended up wedged in the back of the van between the bass player and the singer. Cool Old Biker drove, and the drummer sat shotgun as the van sped down the access road in the deep, dark woods.

Golden Boy was stretched out across Connor's lap, his breathing shallow as he clung to life. Connor noticed his H & S shield logo tattoo peeking through what was left of his torn shirt. It was on his chest, just above his heart and directly below the shredded, bloody mass where his shoulder used to be. Despite the gore and destruction surrounding it, the tattoo still looked perfect and was somehow miraculously intact.

The bass player cradled Golden Boy's head in her lap and gently stroked the side of his face. She almost laughed. "Why didn't you wait for us? You never wait." The moment passed. She snapped out of it and glared at Connor. "Hey, kid."

But Connor couldn't take his eyes off Golden Boy. He could see everything as it was happening in front of him, but it felt dark and watery, like he was watching it happen to someone else on a TV with the brightness turned all the way down.

The bass player said it again, much louder this time, "HEY, KID!" before she punched him in the shoulder significantly harder than she needed to.

Connor winced, then came back. "He stepped in front of me… he doesn't even know me. Why would he do that? Why did he do that? What was that thing? Is he gonna die now—because of me?"

The singer leaned around Connor and looked toward the bass player. "Total brain lock. We're wasting our time."

The bass player shifted toward Connor and placed her hand on his leg, trying to bring him back. "Our friend just saved your life, so now you need to help save his. We need to get him somewhere quiet where we can help him without anyone bothering us. Do you know anywhere like that?"

The van skidded out for a second as it lost traction crossing over from the loose gravel of the access road to the flat pavement of the parking lot. Connor watched The Black Hole speed by through the side window as the van hung a right and blasted back out on to the main road.

The singer shook his head. "Cool story, space cadet."

Connor knew where they could take Golden Boy. It popped into his mind, clear as day. He whispered quietly. "My house."

The singer and the bass player stared at him in unison. The bass player leaned in. "Where?"

Connor blinked and shook himself awake. "My house. My mom is home. But not really. I mean, she won't bother us."

The drummer whipped his phone out in the front seat. "What's your address?"

Connor swallowed. The magnitude of the current situation was sinking in. It was a whole different level to deal with, but there was no turning back now. He owed Golden Boy, if there was still anything left to be done. "1465 Tamarack Street," he said finally.

The drummer typed it into his phone. "Ten miles. Punch it, Limo."

Cool Old Biker nodded and floored it.

The engine groaned. The van's speed spiked rapidly as it rocketed down the empty forest road with nothing but woods and trees on either side for miles…except for the cop car that suddenly whipped out behind them.

The tint of red and blue flashing lights filled the van as the siren wail cut through the still night air. The bass player craned her neck. "Awesome."

The drummer turned back and watched the cop car gain on them through the back window. "What are we doing here, Sarah?"

She thought it over for a few agonizing seconds. "Stop. We gotta. We don't have time, but a high-speed chase doesn't do us any favors. Pull over, Limo."

The van slowed, and Cool Old Biker guided it over on to the soft shoulder of the road. It came to a reluctant stop as he shifted into park.

The cop car skidded to a stop, parked at an angle in front of them and blocked them in. Connor was pretty sure that wasn't a typical maneuver unless the cops were confident something serious was about to go down.

He looked down at Golden Boy, who was torn to pieces and bleeding all over his lap. He had no idea how they were going to plausibly explain any part of what happened, especially since he still didn't understand it himself. He wondered who would take care of his mom when he was sent to prison—or, more likely, the loony bin. This was what he got for going out. He should have just stayed home, like every single other night for the last five years.

The cop one-armed his cruiser door open and sauntered out into the night. Connor eyed the band as they watched the cop approach. They didn't appear nervous, or even the slightest bit concerned; they seemed impatient and inconvenienced, if anything.

The cop flashed a big, over-confident grin as he approached. He blasted two quick, aggressive fingerless whistles, pointed toward the gun currently holstered on his hip, and nodded at the window.

Cool Old Biker and the drummer shared a look in the front seat. Connor could've sworn they were smiling.

The bass player leaned forward between them, "Don't have too much fun. Topper is still bleeding out in the backseat."

As Cool Old Biker reached to roll down the window, his entire body began to change. His skin floated off his body in large sections, far enough for Connor to see the perfect white of his bones underneath. The raised skin shimmered, then swayed and pulsed outward, like ripples on a quiet pond. It changed color and shape… then it rebounded as it pulled back quickly into itself and reattached.

By the time the window was rolled down completely, the cop was staring at his own face. He swayed back, his bravado having suddenly drained down his leg and abandoned him. "What in the country kitchen?" he muttered. Then his jaw just hung there.

The drummer leaned across Cool Old Biker Cop and yelled out the window. "You're stroking out, dude. I know you think you just pulled over a van full of troublemaking kids that you yourself are driving somehow, but in reality you're on the side of the road somewhere with your tongue hanging out of your big, dumb face and your eyes rolled up into the back of your head. So you should probably go sit back in your cruiser until you wake up again—assuming that you do."

The cop nodded dumbly. He stared at "himself" for a few more seconds, then shuffled slowly back to his squad car.

The drummer let out a contented sigh. "Messing with cops never gets old." He turned back to Connor. "1465 Tamarack, right?"

Connor's head lolled forward and he bit down on his tongue. The last thing he was aware of before he passed out was that his mouth was filling with blood.

7

Connor woke up five hours later, covered in someone else's blood.

He was passed out on his kitchen table, the first time he'd ever slept in his favorite room in the house, though it was probably more accurate to say that someone had left him there. He rubbed the side of his face and felt a pair of deep sleep creases that had formed on his cheek. He got up from the table, stretched his legs, and as the flood of last night's events cascaded over him, he realized it was as good a time as any to try and figure out what his missing older brother's all-time favorite punk band was doing in his house.

He peeked through the living room curtains at the van parked in his driveway. He didn't notice a gory crime-scene-level trail of blood leading from the van to his front door. So that was one thing he didn't have to worry about immediately, at least.

He tiptoed back through the living room and down the hallway. The drummer was passed out on the carpet beside the wide-open bathroom door. As Connor carefully stepped over him and into the bathroom, he realized that this was one of the rare instances in life where every single detail of this moment would be seared into his memory forever.

Blood was everywhere—in the sink, and on the toilet; there was a dark, wide path smeared across the floor, and splatters on the wall that crept all the way up to the ceiling. The singer was asleep on the cool, tile floor with his head half-hidden underneath a towel. He almost looked peaceful…except that the entire front of his t-shirt was stained a deep and angry red.

The bass player was sitting up, slumped over with her back against the wall next to the tub. Her legs were pulled into her chest, and her head leaned to the left as it rested against Golden Boy's. They had put him in the tub; and based on all the gauze, medical tape, cotton balls and makeshift tourniquets strewn about the bathroom, Connor could tell they had fought like hell to save him. But he wasn't breathing now and had already started to lose his shine. If Connor had to guess, he had died a few hours earlier.

The bass player opened her eyes. She sat up too quickly, then remembered her friend and reached up to cradle his head a second before it would have smashed against the porcelain tub. She gazed at Golden Boy longingly for a moment and battled to keep it all in before she locked eyes with Connor.

"We need to talk."

-

Connor dropped a tray of fresh pancakes on the kitchen table and took a seat. The band was seated around the table, while Limo stood behind them at the counter and chugged black coffee straight from the pot. The singer reached for the tray and stabbed a few pancakes with his fork. He lifted them up and stared quizzically. "Dinosaurs?"

Connor smiled and let out a soft *rawr*.

The bass player slammed her fist on the table. The singer ignored her, nonplussed, and got to work drowning his pancakes in butter and syrup. But the bass player had Connor's full, undivided attention. She thought for a second while she diagrammed how the conversation should begin.

"Our guitar player died in your bathtub last night," she said as she stared. "He gave himself up for you, which is exactly the type of dumb thing he always does. There are rare people in this world that are made of pure light, love and kindness. Topper was one of the brightest. Not an ounce of malice in his soul. I want to be mad at him for being so virtuous and punch him in his face so goddamn hard it brings him back to life so I can punch him again. But I know he's gone now, and you can't be mad at someone just for being who they are. And that's who he was: he saved people. A lot of them. And if it wasn't for him, you'd be dead right now, and so would I. Only I would have died a long time ago." She paused to catch her breath, like she'd need it for the next part. "His name was Paul Topper, and he was 77 years old. My name is Sarah Hobbes, and believe it or not, I'm 56."

The singer lifted his head up, his mouth full of pancakes. "We all believe it. You totally look like you're 56. Way older, even."

Sarah swatted at him, but he dodged her easily, like it was part of some routine they'd performed a hundred times before.

She nodded at the drummer, and he offered up a cursory little "hello" wave. "Justin Shelby. I was born on the 4th of July in Hazelhurst, Mississippi in 1911. Which makes me 107 years old. I was also supposed to die once, but that was much, much longer ago. I was around long before Topper, so it was someone else who saved me…but that's a story for another day."

Sarah stared at the singer and waited for him to take his turn, but he just kept shoveling pancakes into his mouth until she reached over and snatched his plate away. He stabbed at her with his fork and yelled out with a way-too-full mouth, "I'm still eating." She motioned toward Connor with the plate of pancakes, holding it up as ransom.

The singer licked syrup off his finger. "Lame speech time? Awesome. Alex Frame. Should have died in 1998. Topper saved me too. I'm 36, even though I'll always look 16. Most people would think looking like you're 16 forever is awesome, but I hate it and it's terrible and it makes sure that no one ever takes me seriously about anything. Now please give me back my pancakes, Sarah."

She tossed the plate back down in front of him. Alex wrapped his arm around it protectively and started cutting up the remaining stack of dino parts with the side of his fork. "You guys should really get in on these, by the way. They're fantastic." He stuffed a huge bite into his mouth, then turned to Connor. "How do you get the edges so crispy?"

Connor shifted forward excitedly and an *aww, shucks* grin spread across his lips. His moment has finally arrived. But he couldn't help focusing on Sarah glaring at him. His smile drooped. "That's a story for another day, too."

Sarah shook her head. "Did any of that register with you?"

Connor sighed. "I guess? I mean, I don't understand the joke. Or why it matters if I do."

Sarah leaned back in her chair, picked up a dinosaur pancake, took a huge bite, and chewed thoughtfully. "Because Topper sacrificed himself. FOR YOU. For whatever reason, he chose you. Just like each of us was chosen at some point. Which means you're one of us now."

Connor slowly slid the butter and syrup across the table toward her. "One of what, now?"

Sarah reached for the butter. "Time to shine, Shelbs. Or you know what happens next."

Justin stared at her. "Seriously?"

She nodded excitedly. She was a million percent serious.

Justin whipped around to face Connor. "Okay, kid. Everything that happened after the show last night—how do you explain it?"

Connor thought about it for a second. "Drugs?"

Justin was dumbstruck. "Drugs?!"

Connor nodded. "I mean, I was at a rock concert. There had to be drugs there somewhere. Someone must have dosed me somehow, or they were, like, just in the air or something."

Justin was incredulous. "So you think there are people just walking around rock concerts trying to get random strangers high off of their own very expensive and often hard to come by drugs?"

Connor nodded again. "Pretty much."

Sarah smirked. "Man, kid. I wish that was how it worked."

She grabbed the syrup and held it high in the air, then dowsed her stack of pancakes with it. "Heatseeker isn't just a band. We have songs; we play shows. But that's not the real reason we drive all over the country in our delightful, smelly van. There are things out there, hiding in the dark. Horrible things. Evil things. Just waiting for the chance to sink their rotting teeth into everything bright and hopeful and shiny in the world and rip it all to shreds. It's our job to find those things," she bit the head off her dinosaur pancake for emphasis, "so we can kill them."

Nervous laughter bubbled up out of Connor. "So I guess this is the part where I'm supposed to tell you you're all insane and I don't believe a single thing you just said. Is that how this goes?" But a small, nagging tug in the back of Connor's mind was ready to believe it.

Sarah stood up from her chair, took off her leather jacket, and slowly stretched her arms. "Well, Shelbs. We gave it the old college try."

Justin shook his head. "Come on, Sarah. It takes like two hours to fully reattach, and even after that I have a serious migraine for the rest of the day and I'm super dehydrated."

Sarah shrugged. "Fastest way."

Alex looked up from his pancakes. "Finally!"

Justin inched his chair back from the table deliberately, staring daggers at Connor the entire time. "Let's get it over with."

Sarah stood directly behind Justin, placed her left hand on his left shoulder for leverage, and got a good grip on the left side of his neck with her right hand. She took a breath and grinned at Connor just before digging her fingers into the side of Justin's neck. His skin started to give way, and blood seeped out around Sarah's fingers.

Connor shot back from the table and knocked his chair over on its side.

Sarah grunted as she struggled. "Alex."

Alex stood up from the table and strode toward the stove. He cranked the dial as high as it would go, and a large flame shot up from the front burner. He placed his right hand directly into the flame, and it immediately caught fire. Then he raised his left hand up over his shoulder and opened it wide. A six-inch-tall stream of fire blasted up out of his palm. He kept his right hand over the burner while fire continued shooting out of his left. "Limo?"

Limo set the coffee pot down on the counter, then stared at Connor as his skin floated away from his bones. A second later he was a sickly old woman…then a smiling fat man…then a pouting five-year-old girl…then the alpha cop from last night. Then he was just Cool Old Biker Limo again. He pointed toward Sarah, who was still working hard at decapitating Justin back at the kitchen table.

Connor gazed in horror. Most of the skin around Justin's neck had torn completely away from his shoulders, but Sarah seemed to be having an especially difficult time getting his vertebra to detach. She bit down on bottom her lip, climbed up on Justin's chair for leverage and pulled hard with everything she had.

Justin's spinal cord finally severed with a loud snap. The force launched Sarah from the chair, and she crash-landed on her back on the kitchen floor.

Sarah sat up with a deep, accomplished sigh, then tossed Justin's head on to the kitchen table. It rolled to a stop in the middle. Justin's eyes were wide open, and they immediately found Connor. "Thanks for nothing, kid."

Connor waited for his mind to fracture and what was left of his sanity to burst out the side of his head, leaving a Looney Tunes style sanity-shaped hole as it went, but it didn't happen.

Sarah, Alex, Limo and Justin's head all stared at him quietly. He regarded them thoughtfully. "So I guess you all have superpowers, then."

Connor's mom slowly zombie-walked in from the hallway, dressed in a pair of crusty pajama pants and her missing husband's hockey jersey. Connor rushed over to intercept her before she got too far into the kitchen. "Mom, what are you doing?" But she just stared off into the distance, as blank as ever, and any worry about what she might have just seen instantly faded away. So he turned her around and nudged her gently back toward her room. "I'm just hanging out with some friends, from school," he told her. "That I met, at school. School friends, you know. Anyway, we were just talking, about school, and I was gonna make some breakfast. Why don't you go lay back down and I'll bring you something in."

She padded back down the hallway toward her room and softly croaked out, "That's nice, Connor."

Connor came back into the kitchen just as Sarah lifted Justin's head off the table, placed it back on his shoulders, and gave it a few gruesome twists for good measure. Then Alex closed his left hand, and the flame extinguished. He lifted his right hand up out of the fire, blew it out and clicked the burner back off. He plopped back down at the table, grabbed a few more pancakes with his black-charred hand, and tossed them on to his plate.

Limo walked over to the knife block on the counter, pulled out the boning knife and the butcher knife and held them both up. Sarah nodded at the boning knife, and Limo slid the butcher knife back into the block. Then Limo walked off down the hall, slicing the boning knife back and forth through the air.

Connor followed with his eyes. "What's he doing?"

Justin adjusted his head, trying to get it to sit right. "First of all, Limo is a shapeshifter. And since Limo can transform into anything with a heartbeat, technically Limo isn't a 'he' or a 'she', but more of an 'it'. And don't sweat what Limo's doing. You'll find out in a second."

That did little to soothe Connor's nerves. "She didn't see anything. Honestly. She's not a problem."

Sarah tipped her chair back far enough to snag the coffee pot off the counter, then poured herself some. "I don't care. Ready to listen now?"

Connor nodded and snagged the coffee once Sarah was finished. Something told him he was about to need a serious influx of caffeine.

Sarah dumped a mound of sugar into her coffee. She stirred it slowly, and her spoon scraped against the bottom and the sides of the mug at the same time. "Since the beginning of time, there have always been protectors, guardians whose sole responsibility is to take care of those who don't understand the true depths of evil in the world and would never be able to defend themselves against it anyway. For a long time, they hid in plain sight. They were knights and clerics, scholars and explorers. And wandering musicians. Like us. Which, if you think about it, is actually the perfect cover; traveling from place to place and only staying until the job is done. No one ever asks too many questions or misses you once you're gone, since you're always supposed to go. But evil is tireless, and it's always evolving. Getting bigger, badder, tougher. And we had to, too. So they started grouping us together. Forming bands. Giving us powers. But eventually those powers began to fade, until the day they figured out a way to super-charge them back up. You feel music, deep in your heart—no talking or thinking, just listening and reacting. It's visceral, and an incredibly powerful thing that touches people in a way nothing else can. The crowds believed in us, the wandering musicians. So we harnessed that, and suddenly our shows filled us with energy and made us strong again. But it's different now. We expend so much energy trying to stay anonymous. And people don't believe the way they used to. It's so much harder to engage them now, to get them to look up from their lives for one second and care. So we aren't as strong as we used to be, and there aren't nearly as many of us anymore. But we still do what we can. We show up and play. Charge up and fight. And now, that's your life too."

 Connor felt a heavy hand clamp down on his shoulder. Limo wiped the boning knife clean on his shirt, then dropped it on the table. He carefully pulled a mini H&S Heatseeker Logo badge out from his pocket and it glinted as it caught the light like it was made of metal, but it was caked red with blood around the edges. Connor felt his stomach lurch as he stared at the boning knife and suddenly realized exactly where the badge came from.

 Sarah leaned across the table. "Where do you want it?"

 Connor looked up at her. "I don't suppose 'back where it came from' would be an acceptable answer?"

 Sarah, Justin and Alex conferred and said it practically in unison. "Wrist."

 Limo handed the badge to Justin, then pinned Connor's left arm down on the table. Connor attempted to lift his arm back up, more for the novelty of seeing if he even could than anything else, but Limo's grip felt like hundreds of pounds of solid concrete. Resistance was futile.

He winced as Justin lowered the badge toward his wrist. "Does it hurt?"

Justin shrugged. "Different for everybody."

He pressed the badge softly against the inside of Connor's left wrist. The badge flared and changed color. It flashed a deep, angry orange, as if it were molten, but it felt cool against Connor's skin. He couldn't help but shiver as the sensation traveled up his arm and ricocheted through his body.

The badge sank further, then disappeared as it absorbed into his flesh.

Connor stared at the peach skin on his wrist, then watched as a tiny blue line appeared first. The logo began to fill itself in slowly, in navy blue and bright red ink. It moved back and forth from the top to the bottom, as if some invisible artist were sketching it on him.

In a few seconds it was done, and Connor had his first tattoo.

He held his wrist up and stared in awe. He clenched his fist open and closed a few times and watched it move as the skin loosened and contracted.

Sarah almost laughed. "That's where your power comes from. And as long as you're alive, that's where it stays."

Connor couldn't stop looking at it. Not a single thing about the last sixteen hours felt real, but somehow this part especially. He had stared at the logo for countless hours in Sam's room but never imagined seeing it on his own skin. He wasn't sure how any of this was supposed to work, but placebo effect or not, he swore he already felt different.

He finally forced his wrist down and looked up at the band. "I have many, many questions."

Sarah poured more coffee. "Shoot."

"What's my power?"

Justin responded. "We don't know. Yet. The badge reacts to everyone differently and it typically takes a few days before you'll start to feel it. But if I had to guess, you probably won't be that far off from Topper."

Connor nodded, as if that was a perfectly normal and acceptable explanation. "What could Topper do?"

Justin thought about his friend and couldn't help but smile. "He was an empath. He could touch you and read everything about you—your emotions, your feelings…your memories. Your past."

Connor remembered the sensation he felt when Topper put his hands on him in the woods the night before—how all his fear disappeared and suddenly he felt calm and at peace, despite everything that was happening. Being able to do that for someone else wouldn't be so bad.

Connor asked Justin, "What's yours?"

Justin gestured toward the torn skin on his neck as it slowly conjoined. "Regeneration through accelerated healing. Tear me into a hundred pieces and I'll grow back. Which makes me kind of invincible I guess."

Connor pointed at Sarah. "Yours?"

Sarah stood from the table, picked up Limo and put him over her shoulder. She scooped up Justin and tossed him on top of Limo. Then she lifted up Alex with her other hand, chair and all, and balanced him in the air. She answered loud and clear, without a hint of struggle in her voice. "Strength." She dropped them all on the kitchen floor in a big pile then took her seat again.

Alex got up on a knee, then dug his elbows into the table and pulled himself up. "So hilarious. Every time." He sat back down at the table and turned toward Connor. "I absorb energy—thermal, chemical, electromagnetic; kinetic, sonic, um…gravitational. Physical strength in certain scenarios. And when I concentrate hard enough and nobody messes with me, *Sarah*, I can redirect it back out. Like you saw with the fire. It's hard, though. It makes me super tired. Plus I'm always starving." Alex grabbed the tray with last few remaining dinosaur pancakes, as if to illustrate his point. "Anybody else want these?" He didn't even wait for a response before he stuffed an entire pancake in his mouth.

Connor looked back to Sarah and Justin. "Does Limo do anything besides shapeshifting?"

Justin and Sarah traded a glance before Justin took a stab at it. "It never sleeps or gets tired. It always wants to drive; hence the name. It just kind of showed up one day. We assume they sent it to help us, but since it doesn't talk, it can't really tell us. And I guess we've never really bothered to ask."

Connor's brow furrowed. "Ask who?"

Sarah jumped in. "We have help. I mean, we're not just out here on our own picking towns at random in hopes of finding some kind of ancient evil we can rough up. We're part of a network, The Underground, that's been around for a very long time. It keeps us connected to everyone else who's still fighting and gives us help and information when we need it."

Connor was beginning to see the line now. "So like, where to play? And what'll be out there waiting when you're done?"

Sarah nodded.

And now Connor had to ask, even though he was positive he didn't want to know. "So what was that thing that got Topper?"

Sarah shook her head. "A Death Wolf. We'd never even heard of it until two days ago, and as far as they know, it's the only one. Every few years it comes out for a feeding cycle then disappears. Which means we've only got a few days left to stop it."

Connor swallowed hard. "And how are we supposed to do that?"

The question hung there unanswered, lingering over their heads until Connor's front door flew open and Nina busted in.

She was already talking before she was even fully inside. "Quikstuff, why is Heatseeker's van parked in your driveway?" She entered the kitchen and froze dead in her tracks. Her mouth dropped and hung open as she just stared.

Alex leaned over to Connor. "Is she broken?"

Connor shrugged.

Alex wadded up the last remaining pancake, then chucked it at Nina. It was a direct hit that caught her in the forehead and snapped her right out of it. Her entire face flushed. "Hi, Heatseeker. Just hanging out in Quikstuff's kitchen." She bent down and picked up the pancake, then unwadded it and took a bite. "Why are you here?"

They all looked at each other. Justin opened his mouth to respond, but he had nothing. Sarah jumped in. "Your friend…" She locked eyes with Connor and suddenly realized she had no idea what his name was. "…FNG."

Nina's nose scrunched. "FNG?"

Justin sighed. "Effing New Guy."

Connor chimed in. "Or, you know, Connor. Like my actual name. Which is Connor."

Sarah shook her head slowly. "Through an unforeseen set of circumstances, most of which were the result of his own doing, FNG officially became our new guitar player last night."

Nina frowned. "Connor Quikstadt is your new guitar player? This kid, right here? Connor?"

Sarah nodded and tried to sell it. "He's just…so good."

Nina scoffed. "I have never, not once *ever*, heard what I can only imagine would be truly terrible guitar playing coming from this house. But suddenly Connor plays guitar?"

Connor didn't play guitar, not even once in his life. He was always too afraid to try Sam's for fear he would somehow instantly break it. That part of the equation hadn't dawned on him yet.

Nina was even more dubious. "What happened to the other guy?"

They all glanced down the hallway toward the bathroom.

Justin smiled softly. "It was time for him to move on. I think he'd been looking for a reason to leave for a long time."

Nina clapped Connor on the shoulder. "Well, come on then, rock god. Bust out your guitar. Play me some Heatseeker."

Justin got up. "It's the one hanging in your room, right? The Hagstrom?"

Justin turned to go, but Connor grabbed his arm. "That's not my room. It's someone else's. And that's their guitar too. Besides, it doesn't work. Maybe later, Nina."

Nina's face lit up. "How about tonight? You know, Faraz's dad is out of town and we're having this huge party at his house. You should play. It could be your first show with your new band that you're definitely the guitar player in, Connor. I think everyone will want to see that."

Connor shook his head. "Nina, I don't think—"

Sarah cut him off. "We're in."

Nina cracked a slightly evil smile. "Heatseeker. At Faraz's dad's. I gotta go call Marissa, and Fragile Dave, and Bailey, and tell them to get the word out. No one will believe this. It's gonna be a packed house tonight, Connor. That's for sure."

8

Connor was wedged between Sarah and Alex in the back seat of the van again, in the exact same spot as last night, but this time every ounce of his attention was focused on the tarp stuffed under the seat. They hadn't made him help roll up Topper's body, but all of them had to work together for a solid three hours to clean up the blood in the bathroom after they'd carried it out to the van. Every time Limo hit a bump, Connor was sure the tarp was going to unfurl itself somehow and Topper's cold, dead body would come tumbling out. So he distracted himself by staring out the window as Evergreen passed by.

He realized now just how much the town was ingrained into every fiber of his being. Everything about him began and ended there. It was his entire world, all he had ever known. And now that he was spending time with people who weren't from there—essentially for the first time ever—it's worn-down appearance and lack of character made him feel self-conscious and incredibly small.

If he believed everything they told him back in his kitchen (and he still wasn't entirely sure that he did), they ranged in age from 36 to 107 years old and had spent the better part of their lives driving all over the country, playing rock shows, having adventures and killing monsters. What the hell did he possibly have to talk to them about?

Without realizing it, Sarah helped him out. "Since your house is home base for the moment, are there any more of your friends we're gonna have to worry about busting in the front door and getting in our business?"

Connor barely needed time to consider the question before he offered up a resounding, "Nope."

Sarah nodded. "Any plans coming up? Any friends you're gonna have to avoid or dodge? We can help you come up with a cover story. We're pretty good at it by now."

Alex leaned over. "Especially Sarah. She's exceptionally full of crap."

Sarah lunged behind Connor to slug Alex, but Alex pulled a classic little brother counter and scooted just beyond her reach.

Connor shook his head. "I'm cool."

Sarah and Alex shared a concerned glance behind his back. "So you don't have any friends that we need to be concerned about?"

Connor sat back in his seat. "Nope. No friends to worry about at all."

-

"Can I, for one, say how overwhelmingly excited I am to be back in the woods?" Alex adjusted his glasses as he stepped out of the van and out into the forest. They were parked on the old deserted access road again, not too far from where they'd been last night. He wheeled on Sarah as she and Connor climbed out behind him. "How long is this gonna take? I swear to God, I'm so hungry I'm about to eat my own face off."

Justin jumped down from the front passenger seat. "Maybe not the best statement given recent events."

Alex shrugged. "Whatever. Doesn't come out until after dark anyway, right?"

Sarah nodded. "All our info says it's nocturnal. So we should be good."

Connor couldn't help but focus on the *should be* part of that sentence.

Limo walked around the back of the van and joined them.

Sarah pointed out toward the woods. "Scout it out?" Limo nodded rapidly. It was the first time Connor had seen it get genuinely excited about anything. Then it shapeshifted into a goofy, slobbery, floppy-eared Golden Retriever and sprinted off as fast as its legs would take it.

Connor's expression exploded in amazement. He looked back and forth quickly from Sarah to Alex to Justin and waited for someone to confirm that what he just saw was, in fact, real.

Justin grinned. "Anything with a heartbeat."

Alex shook his head. "Yeah. Super awesome, until the first time you see it take a dump."

Sarah rounded them up. "Shelbs, you and FNG search west. Me and the fecal master will head east. Limo will let us know if it finds anything. We're looking for its lair—that's it." She stared daggers at Connor. "Stay out the way. Stay out of trouble. Listen to Justin. You're no good to us until your powers are up and running. And maybe not even then. If you find anything, scream your head off and we'll find you."

Sarah opened the back of the van and pulled two packs out. She tossed one at Justin. "The only thing that matters right now is finding where it lives. There'll be plenty of time for payback later. Believe me."

-

Connor felt like they had been walking forever.

He didn't really know what he was supposed to be looking for, but at some point the repetitive scenery mixing with the rhythmic cracking of the dried brush beneath their feet put him into some sort of deep hypnosis. He practically walked right into Justin before he realized that he'd stopped.

Justin dropped to a knee, grabbed a long, skinny branch and sifted through a pile of dead foliage in the open base of a giant sequoia. Once he was confident there was no secret Death Wolf passageway hidden beneath the leaves, he stood up and started walking again. Connor lagged behind, still wandering through his haze.

Justin glanced back. "You okay?"

Connor shook his head to will the cobwebs away. "When I was little I used to turn my lights off at bedtime then sprint across my room as fast as I could to jump into bed before the monsters could get me. One night when I was six, I slipped on a Micro Machine and broke my arm. I remember my parents sitting me down on my bed and telling me there were no such things as monsters. Swearing to me up and down…they don't exist; they aren't real. And I believed them. Never had a reason not to up until this morning. So all of this, it's just…a lot."

Justin knew it was. He drifted back to the moment when everything changed for him and tried to recall what that new weight on his brain felt like. But his circumstances were much different. It had been so long ago, and he'd been through so much since then, he wasn't entirely sure he could remember it accurately anymore. But that was how it went for a lot of things these days. And one day soon, that would go for Topper as well; he'd be just another name on a list that kept getting longer, people who Justin had outlived and eventually faded out of his memory. That stung him somewhere deep. He gritted his teeth and took a sharp breath to try and make it go away.

He eased back on his pace and fell into stride with Connor. He couldn't believe how young Connor was. Yesterday, he was just some normal kid, and now all of that had been taken away from him. So he decided it was the perfect time for a peace offering.

"I can fix that Hagstrom for you, if you want," Justin said. "You'd be surprised how good you get at fixing guitars when you've been playing in bands for ninety years."

Connor's answer flew out of his mouth and sounded much harsher than he intended it to. "Don't touch that guitar. Ever. The experience of fixing it belongs to someone else."

Justin could practically feel Connor begging him to ask. Still, he took extra care to gauge how much runway the kid would give him. "Who does it belong to?"

Connor softened. His flash of anger dissipated, and he answered barely above a whisper. "My brother, Sam."

Justin nodded thoughtfully. "Where is he?"

Connor's head drooped. "I don't know. Him and my dad went out one Saturday morning and never came back. I don't know what they were doing. I don't know where they went. But he's out there somewhere. I know it. I can still feel him. Every day."

Justin stayed quiet for a few seconds, letting Connor's feelings breathe. "My brother was the only one who ever really looked out for me," he told Connor. "For a long time it was just the two of us against the world, until one day it wasn't anymore. And then he was gone. Forever. I still feel that. Every day. There's a wavelength that exists between brothers that binds you in a way nothing else can. So trust your gut, if that's what you feel. If there's one person who would know for sure, it's you. And if you say he's still out there somewhere, I believe you. Maybe I can even help you find him one day."

Connor wiped at his eyes with his sleeve. Before the moment completely overtook him, there was a loud cracking of heavy branches behind them. Something big was coming through the brush and closing in fast.

Justin instinctively stepped in front of Connor. His eyes darted back and forth from Connor's terrified face to the trees as he tried to discern where the van was. He knew he only had a few seconds to decide: fight or flight. But it wasn't a legitimate question at that point. Connor would be zero help; they wouldn't stand a chance.

He grabbed Connor by the shoulders and screamed in his face. "Run!"

Then he shoved Connor forward and sprinted as hard as he could behind him. He dug his forearm into Connor's back and forced him onward as fast as their legs would go.

Justin felt his breath shorten, but he had to waste some of what little he had left. He raised his head and shouted into the trees as loud as he could. "SARAH!!! ALEX!!! VAN!!!" It rang out through the still forest air. He hoped it would carry far enough to make a difference.

There was a flash of movement in front of them. Just as Justin was about to yank Connor to a halt, the Golden Retriever came barreling out of the bushes straight toward them. Limo skidded out and turned around quickly. Then it took off like a rocket, dashed ahead and lead them back out of the woods.

Justin and Connor burst through the tree line, their feet hitting the solid, packed dirt of the access road. The van was parked a few hundred feet away. They ran hard for it, using up whatever energy they had left.

Sarah and Alex sprinted out of the woods from the opposite side of the road up ahead. Connor's nerves rose another level once he saw how concerned Sarah was as she watched them running scared. She crouched down in front of the van, rooted through her pack, pulled a red road flare out from inside, ripped the top off and sparked it. It caught fire and hissed.

Alex dropped his left hand just above Sarah's head. She stabbed the flare up into his palm and held it there. Connor could swear he smelled Alex's skin melting as they closed in.

But Alex didn't waver; his focus stayed locked on the tree line behind them. He balled his right fist up, and it glowed brighter and brighter, as if it was charging up.

Justin and Connor finally reached the van and slid down behind Sarah and Alex for cover. Limo was further down the road, barking angrily at whatever was headed their way. They stared and waited for a few agonizing seconds, Alex fully charged and ready to fire.

Then two 13-year-old boys slowly ambled out of the woods, pushing three bikes. The boy in front, the obvious leader of the two, wore a vintage royal-blue Mariners hat. He pushed two bikes by himself…one of which was Connor's. He dropped them both in the dirt the second he noticed Sarah scorching Alex's hand off.

"Badass!" he said. "That's a thirty-minute spikeless waxed flare. Burns up to twenty-nine hundred degrees Fahrenheit, hot enough to burn bone, and you're just holding it on dude's hand like it's Sunday morning. Are you guys in some kind of cult or something? Because me and Wade could probably be convinced to join if you are." The kid nodded at Sarah. "Especially if I get to sit next to you at the meetings."

Sarah and Alex were so busy staring at the boy, it took them a few seconds to remember what they were doing. Sarah stood up quickly and hurled the still-burning flare up the road while Alex jammed his left hand under his right arm and tried to smother it.

The kids just smiled. "I'm not down with weird cult names though. Wade is like, who cares? But I'm named Henry, and that's after my grandpa. So it's non-negotiable."

Connor walked forward and reached for his bike, but Henry hustled over and stomped it back down. Henry sized Connor up. "What're you doing?"

Connor backed up a little. "That's my bike."

Henry shook his head. "We found it in the woods."

Connor tried to skirt around Henry and get back to his bike. "Yeah. Because I left it here last night."

Henry nodded. "What were you doing out here last night? Cult stuff?"

Connor tried to sound cool and dangerous as he brushed past Henry. "You couldn't handle it if I told you." Henry's friend Wade stepped forward and stood directly in front of the bikes.

Sarah rolled her eyes. "Seriously." She lunged forward and lifted both of the 13-year-olds up by their shirts. Then she tossed them both, a little too hard and a little too far, and they landed on their asses in the middle of the road.

Henry scrambled to his feet. "I don't wanna sit next to you at the meetings anymore."

Justin sighed. "There isn't any cult."

Henry thought it over. "So she was just burning that guy's hand with that flare for fun?"

Justin shrugged at Sarah. "Valid question."

Sarah deadpanned, "He had a tic on him."

Henry obviously wasn't buying it. So Alex walked up and waved his good-as-new hand in Henry's face. "No burns. See. Just a regular, boring hand."

Then Alex bent down, snatched Connor's bike and dragged it back toward the van. "Let's go. I'm starving." Henry opened his mouth to protest, but he knew it didn't matter anymore. Limo trotted back down the road and jumped up into the van after Alex.

Henry smiled at Sarah. "That your dog? I'm a dog person too. We can be friends again."

She glared back. "No."

Justin leaned in toward Henry. "Our turn for questions. What are you doing out here?"

Henry picked his bike up and brushed it off. "We come out here to blow stuff up. Wade got a bunch of quarter sticks for his birthday last week and we were about to…" Henry glared at Connor, "…tie them to this janky bike we found and blow the crap out of it until this skinny dude came along and started whining about how it was his bike, and then his lame friends who are definitely in a cult stole it from us, and now I'm talking to this old guy and explaining every single thing to him because apparently he has nothing better to do."

Sarah took a step closer to Henry. "You know, if you were just a few years older, I'd…"

Henry grinned. "You'd what?"

Sara grinned back. "Beat you to a pulp."

But Henry wasn't thrown, and he held her stare. "You're the wildcard, huh? I like that."

Sarah almost smiled but caught herself. She glanced at Justin. "We should head for the show."

As she turned and headed for the van, Henry yelled after her. "What show?" Once it was clear Sarah wasn't going to answer, he turned to Justin and Connor instead. "What show?"

Connor wanted to earn back some cool points. "We're in a band. We're playing a house party tonight."

Henry nodded. "My sister is going to that."

Connor had to know. "Who's your sister?"

Henry glared at him, still pissed about the bike. "Marissa Spooner."

Connor shook his head. *Of course*, he thought.

Henry caught Connor's reaction. "What? You know her?"

Connor pulled back, not wanting to get into it with Henry. "I live next door to Nina, so I see her a lot. Probably more often than either one of us would like."

Henry pointed at Connor. "I know you now. You're that weird, sad kid."

Justin put his arm around Connor. "Time to go." He nudged him softly toward the van. "I'll be there in a second."

Justin turned back to Henry and Wade. "We're headed out. You probably should too, because—"

Henry cut him off. "My parents have been warning me about these woods since I was little. The only reason we're out here is because it's the only place in this hick-ass town where no one bothers us. I know you think you're safe because you're all weird and culty and stuff, but you're not. Bad stuff happens here. You can feel it in your bones. So next time you think about coming back, don't."

9

"I think this is the place."

Cool Old Biker Limo pulled the van over to the side of the street as Justin held up his phone. The flashing blue dot on the screen had just arrived in his GPS app.

Justin glanced back for confirmation but Connor just shrugged. "I've never been here before."

Alex looked out the side window, laughed and shook his head. "Yeah. This is it."

They all whipped around just in time to see a few kids cheering on a girl as she puked her guts out into the lilac bushes in front of the house.

Alex clapped Connor on the back. "Guess kids get started a little early around here, huh?"

Connor squinted through the window to get a good look at the girl's face. He recognized her immediately. It was Kaitlyn Bouse;

she and Connor had gone to school together since kindergarten. Connor had always felt bad for Kaitlyn. She was an outsider, like him…only different. Kaitlyn was overweight and saddled with navigating her childhood with a last name that conveniently rhymed with *house*. As if that wasn't enough, her older brother Jason was a drug-dealing burnout who didn't care about anything, let alone normal teenage behavior like going to school, practicing personal hygiene, and not telling people they should kill themselves every five seconds. Conner had watched Kaitlyn be crushed under the weight of all this the moment they started high school. Jason was such a phenomenal screw up, in fact, that every possible prejudice that could be applied to their family name had become the gospel on Kaitlyn before she'd ever even stepped foot through the front doors of good ol' Westerberg High. And so, she'd given in, embraced that destiny and become what everyone expected her to be: the girl who would be forever puking on someone else's front porch before the party even started, while the dickheads filmed it on their phones, just in case the railing broke.

    Connor had zero doubt her brother was off somewhere else, puking into an entirely different set of bushes at that very same moment.

    Sarah snapped her fingers in Connor's face. "Showtime."

    Everyone else was already outside the van, waiting.

-

    Connor had been in the bathroom for twenty-seven minutes now.

    When they came in the house, it was just Faraz and a small cluster of burnouts Connor barely knew, spread out around the kitchen table chugging lukewarm Rainier tallboys and doing shots of Fireball. Connor's plan was to head off to the bathroom to have his massive freak-out alone. Then he'd splash some water on his face, as cold as the tap would go, and get it together just long enough to sneak back out of the bathroom and try to escape from the party, knowing full well that they'd bust him and drag him up on stage, and his eternal humiliation would be complete.

But when he put his hand on the doorknob the first time and tried his best to trick his brain into believing he was actually going to open it, he heard a considerable rise in both the volume and number of voices coming from the other side. There were more people out there now. A lot more.

With each subsequent standoff among his hand, his self-esteem and the knob, the mythical crowd expanded exponentially in his mind, and what lay on the other side of the door became infinitely more terrifying. The house and the party were an entirely different organism than the one he had left. He would be walking out into a brand-new world now. People were there to see *him*, full of expectations.

A fist pounded hard on the door, three times in rapid succession. Connor jumped so quickly he almost slipped his skin.

Whoever was on the other side waited barely a few seconds before they knocked again—twice, and even harder. Connor realized he no longer had a choice to make. He reached for the knob and turned it slowly, resigned to his fate.

Marissa leaned against the wall with a Cheshire Cat grin on her face. He could tell immediately from the look in her eyes that she knew he was hiding out in the bathroom alone, and that she got an extra-special charge being the one to chase him out. He wondered if she'd been listening at the door and how long she'd waited before she'd knocked.

Connor tried to slip past her. "Hey, Marissa."

She slid over and sealed him in. "Sad Sack."

Connor stared at her uncomfortably for a few agonizing seconds, waiting for her to unsheathe her claws and put him out of his misery. She leaned in close enough for him to feel the heat from her breath on the side of his cheek. "Faraz may feel sorry enough for you to fall for this charade," she said, "but I don't. And neither does Nina, or anyone else. Whatever this is, it's all about to explode in your face… and after it does, no one will ever feel sorry for you again."

Connor closed his eyes and swallowed hard, trying to drag all his fear down into the deepest part of his gut, to drown it. But it exploded up like a depth charge instead and violently forced everything out in its wake.

He lurched forward, pressed against Marissa's shoulder, leaned in, and spoke directly. "You're right. I can't play guitar. Like, at all. And I'm supposed to go stand in front of a room full of people I've known my entire life, with a band I barely know, and I have no idea what's gonna happen. It's too late now; I can't turn back. I can't run away and hide anymore, even though that's the only thing I'm actually good at. For years, I've told myself I was fine on my own; I didn't need any friends and I didn't care what people thought about me. I've lived on that lie for years because it's the only thing that keeps me from going insane. But here's the truth: I care so goddamned much what everyone thinks that I'm about to go nuclear. This is the first time in a very long time that anyone has expected anything from me, and I'm terrified because I know I'm gonna blow it. So congratulations. You got me. You win, Marissa. Happy now?"

Marissa took a deliberate step back and stared hard at Connor, waiting a few seconds to make sure he registered the look on her face and the fact that none of what he'd just said changed anything as far as she was concerned. "See you out there."

She let the words tumble out of her mouth as she turned and walked away.

-

Connor felt every set of eyes in the living room as they bored into his back. He dropped to one knee and noodled with Topper's Orange guitar amp for the fifth time in two minutes, trying his best to look like he had some vague idea of what he was supposed to be doing. But he was beyond lost, and with every hesitation he waited for someone to finally scream out "POSER!" and start handing out torches and pitchforks.

He heard an excited squeal rise above the steady volume of party noise from somewhere in the back of the living room, and he knew that Nina had arrived without even turning to look. He'd hoped somehow she wouldn't get there in time to witness his demise.

Cool Old Biker Limo dropped the guitar case at Connor's feet. Connor craned his neck and offered his best, most pathetic *Please, Help Me!* face.

Limo knelt down next to Connor, and in a matter of seconds managed to correctly plug in the amp's power cord (which Connor had been unsuccessfully trying to shove into the instrument cable input), insert one instrument cable into the correct input, plug that cable into the distortion pedal, and run another cable from the distortion pedal going out.

It held the cable out for Connor to take, but Connor shook his head adamantly and whispered, "Can you play guitar?"

Limo unsheathed the 1964 Sunburst Fender Telecaster, which technically now belonged to Connor, and plugged it in. Instantly, it let out an angry screech of ungodly feedback, almost on cue, as if it wanted to ensure that anyone who'd previously been enjoying the party and not staring directly at Connor would now be giving him their full, undivided attention.

Limo stood, tugged Connor up beside him, and slid the guitar strap over Connor's shoulder while the young man grimaced out all his feelings in return. Then Limo gave him a happy, almost childlike little wave as he backed up into the crowd and disappeared into the sea of teenagers.

Justin walked out from behind his drums and adjusted a cymbal stand, then leaned in close and whispered to Connor. "Everything alright?"

Connor blinked rapidly and answered way too loudly. "It feels like all the blood in my body has turned to sugar and now I want to puke five thousand times. Can you hold this?"

He started to take off the guitar and hand it to Justin.

Justin shook his head. "Why?"

Connor tried to force him to take it. "Because I'm gonna go puke five thousand times."

Sarah strode over, yanked the guitar strap back down onto Connor's shoulder and whisper-hissed at him, "You've spent enough time in the bathroom tonight." She released Connor and stared him down before she headed back to her bass rig. Alex unzipped his hoodie and wrapped it neatly around the base of the mic stand as the crowd of teenagers watched the band's every move. There was a palpable storm cloud of anticipation and energy building in the air. They could feel it was almost time.

Nina caught Connor's eye from the back of the living room. She was standing with Marissa, Faraz, Fragile Dave, Bailey and a bunch of other super-cool looking people he was about to embarrass himself in front of.

Connor twisted around quickly, dropped his head and stared down at the guitar. He didn't know what to do, so he just stayed really still. He guessed he would be in this exact spot in Faraz's dad's living room for the rest of his life now. He felt large, stinging tears build up behind his eyes, and he knew he only had a few seconds until they forced their way through.

Alex wrapped his arm around Connor and gave him a half body hug as Justin dropped to a knee and slid into his eyeline. "What's going on, kid?"

Connor sniffled. "I don't even know how to hold this stupid thing. It's so heavy. I hate it. I'm fine with people looking through me. I'm used to that. But once they start laughing at me? There's no coming back."

Alex and Justin shared a concerned look. Then Justin suddenly got it. "Wait…you don't know how to play guitar?"

Connor nodded.

Justin's hand shot to his mouth in recognition. "The Hagstrom… it's your brother's guitar. Dude. I'm so sorry. We never even thought to ask."

Alex rested his hand on the crown of Connor's head and gently touched his forehead to Connor's. "We wouldn't do that to you, dude. Ever. You're one of us. All you have to do is let go. Trust the badge. We got the rest."

Connor felt the mountain of weight crushing his chest begin to float away. "So I don't need to know how to play guitar?"

Justin tilted his hand back and forth. "I mean, it helps. But not really."

Now Connor felt even lighter. "So Topper didn't know how to play guitar, either?"

Alex shook his head. "Oh, no. Topper was a beast."

Justin nodded in agreement. "Yeah. Easily the best I've ever seen. And I've played with a hundred and forty-two guitar players."

Alex patted Connor on the back for good measure. "You got this. Don't sweat it."

Then he turned, grabbed the mic and stared out at the crowd. "What's up, Evergreen! Nice to see you again."

The crowd went nuts.

Sarah tossed her bass over her shoulder as Justin slid in behind the drums. Alex barked into the mic. "We're called Heatseeker. I believe you know our good friend, Connor. Be gentle, it's his first show. He's gonna start it off tonight."

Every ounce of attention was laser-focused on Connor once again. He stared out at them, frozen in place. The dead air began to gain weight and the silence dragged on long enough that sharpened murmurs of annoyance started rippling through the room of half-wasted teenagers.

Alex covered the microphone with his hand and leaned over to Connor. "You just gotta start. Trust me. Your instincts will take over."

The problem was that Connor's instincts currently told him to go buy some hair dye, find a gas station bathroom, and run off to start a new life somewhere. So he did what he'd always done when felt lost and alone and scared.

He closed his eyes and thought about Sam.

A calm took over his body. Connor felt it pass into his temples and spread slowly down through his shoulders, along his spine, into his stomach and down his legs until eventually all the fear and tension in his body released and dissipated completely.

When Connor opened his eyes, he had already started playing without even realizing it. While no one would ever confuse his guitar playing with Topper's in a million years, he was surprised by how natural it felt. It was choppy and clumsy, but there was an undercurrent of confidence.

He couldn't remember Heatseeker playing whatever song was coming out of him now, but there was no way he could stop it even if he wanted to. It was on the loose and ready to attack with it's teeth out.

Connor played faster and louder, strumming so hard it felt like his shoulder was about to dislocate.

Alex, Sarah and Justin shared a quick glance. They were in uncharted territory for the first time in years and it woke up something in each of them they hadn't even realized they'd been missing.

When Alex started screaming out the brand new words, Connor screamed right along with him. And then he felt the Earth shake as the entire world changed beneath his feet.

-

Connor was a maniac.

While a slight overshoot was to be expected when dealing with a massive course correction, Connor seemed to have let go of everything that had been holding him back, so completely and thoroughly that he'd blown right past the normal teenage rebellion phase and tapped into something full-on primal. Countless kids who knew Connor from school would spend the rest of the night telling each other they'd never seen that side of Connor before, and it would be extra, even-more-than-usual true. Because until tonight, this particular side of Connor did not exist.

The band was killing it, and he was doing so well he could swear he almost saw Sarah smile at one point.

It was somewhere toward the middle of the sixth song when Connor saw him standing by himself in the back of the crowd: a man, far too grown-up to blend in at a teenage house party. He was an entire head taller than everyone else and dressed in a black, high-end designer suit. Connor focused on him without even realizing it, cornered by his own curiosity. The swarm of writhing, sweaty, teenage bodies parted just wide enough for Connor to see the man's hands and what they were doing.

They were *glowing*.

The man pushed through the crowd slowly, headed straight toward Connor.

Connor wanted to look around and see if anyone else had noticed the man. But for some reason, he couldn't break his gaze, no matter how hard he tried.

The man's hands were white-hot now and getting brighter by the second. They grew so bright that Connor's eyes started to water. His reflexes took hold, and he squeezed them shut.

When he opened them up again, the man was staring directly at him from a few feet away.

And smiling.

The man drew both his glowing fists back to his sides and held them steady. Locked and loaded, he dropped his head and took aim. Then his arms exploded forward, launching a sonic boom of energy headed directly for Connor.

Alex caught the sudden movement out of the corner of his eye at the last second and leapt in front of Connor. The stream of energy blasted Alex in the chest and sent him careening into Justin's drum set.

And now, everyone else noticed the man too, all at once.

Alex sprang up off Justin's drums, his t-shirt burned and his chest smoking. He glared at the man, but the man wasn't thrown in the slightest. He gave Alex the tiniest nod, as if politely encouraging him to do something about it, should he feel so inclined.

Alex cocked his right fist back as far as it could go, then shot it forward and released the sonic boom of energy right back.

The man blew through the crowd and slammed into the back wall of the living room so hard and with such force that he broke completely through the drywall and most of the way through the other layers underneath.

The man stood up, his back somehow unbroken, and gently dusted himself off. He opened his mouth to speak, but Sarah charged forward and punched him squarely in the face with everything she had. The man flew through whatever was left of the wall. A few kids poked their heads through the hole just in time to see him rise to his feet, sprint out of the backyard, and disappear into the night.

Alex gave Connor a once-over. "You alright?"

Connor nodded. "I think so. Thank you."

A drunken rando from the back yelled out, "WHAT THE HELL WAS THAT?!"

Sarah rejoined Connor, Alex and Justin. They all stared at each other blankly. "Part of the show?" Justin deadpanned.

Faraz pushed his way through the crowd and stared at the gaping hole that used to be his father's living room wall. "Oh my God," he whispered. A wave of silent apprehension passed through the crowd as everyone started to mentally calculate the massive ass beating he was sure to receive. Faraz's eyes darted through his friends and back up to the band before his face broke into a huge smile. "That was awesome!"

A flurry of fists flew up into the air and the room exploded with cheers as the tension vanished.

Sarah nodded at Justin as he climbed back behind the drums and picked up his sticks. He held them up above his head and counted off. "One, two, three, four!"

-

Connor, Alex, Sarah and Justin were huddled together behind the hot tub as it bubbled away. Their faces changed color every few seconds in unison with the timed pattern of strobing LEDs hidden beneath the water. The rest of the partygoers, including Nina and her crew, stood a good hundred and fifty feet away, crammed around the keg and gawking at the band in quiet wonder.

Connor looked in their direction, gave them all a cursory nod and turned back uncomfortably. "So what the hell was that?" he whispered sharply.

Alex shrugged. "Beats me. But at least Super Sarah didn't punch Johnny Businessman though this bad boy." He knocked on the side of the hot tub. "Because I'm definitely taking a soak once I find something to eat. Plus, that kid's dad would have murdered him."

Justin and Sarah were far more concerned. Sarah's brow furrowed. "I think he was from Corporate."

Alex squinted dismissively. "No way."

Justin nodded. "Makes sense."

Alex shook his head. "Get out of town!" They all stared at him. "Just wanted to make sure that you're listening."

Connor needed to know. "What's Corporate?"

Justin's dour expression matched his response. "You know how we're the good guys and we have people looking out for us? Well, the bad guys do too. We call them Corporate—as in Evil Incorporated. Like, literally. We've heard stories about their 'operatives' for years but we've never seen any sign that they actually existed. So it would be a wee bit concerning if one of them just showed up out of the blue to target us. That would mean something has put us on their radar."

Justin, Sarah and Alex all stared at Connor.

Connor shrank. "Or, you know, the Dead Wolf is super important and he's here to protect it?"

"Death Wolf." Alex laughed. "And Wall Street just tried to flame-broil you specifically."

Sarah turned to Justin. "Reach out. See if you can find out what this means. Is it because we have a weak link now?" Sarah glanced at Connor, letting him know this was exactly what she thought it was. "Or is it something more than that? In the meantime…this is getting weird."

Sarah nodded toward the crowd staring at the band. They tried their best not to be obvious about it but failed miserably.

She squeezed past Justin and abandoned their hot tub sanctuary. "Time to mix it up." She approached the crowd, and they parted like the Red Sea. She grabbed a plastic Solo cup and filled it from the keg as everyone watched in complete silence. Then she lifted the cup to salute, chugged it, and climbed back into the house through the gigantic hole in the wall.

-

Connor wondered if this was what life was always like for popular kids.

Everywhere he went in the house, someone wanted a moment with him to share some anecdote that connected them—the first time they met, or the first class they had together, or how they always knew he was cool by the way he was so confident in keeping to himself. Everything had changed now, and the constant stream of attention was exhausting and weirded him out. He grabbed the 1964 Sunburst Fender Telecaster, crept off down the hall and snuck into the first room he came across. Suddenly, playing guitar was the only thing he felt like doing.

He nudged the door open and walked in just in time to see a shirtless Faraz spray a giant mist of cologne up into the air and take a curious whiff. If he was bothered that Connor had shown up in his bedroom, he didn't show it. And he didn't seem to be self-conscious that Connor saw him with his shirt off, either, which somehow felt like the weirdest thing Connor had experienced so far. He couldn't imagine ever taking his shirt off in front of anybody.

Faraz sprayed the bottle dangerously close to Connor and asked, "What does this smell like to you?"

Connor leaned in slightly, careful not to get any of it on him. "Like somebody microwaved a burrito diaper?"

Faraz shook his head. "It's supposed to smell like leather and tree moss with a subtle hint of lavender. I spent seventy bucks on this stuff! Think your bass player will like it?"

That definitely took Connor by surprise. "Sarah?" he blurted out. "I'm pretty sure she doesn't like anything."

Faraz smirked. "Not even fly-as-hell, super-mature-for-their-age, five-foot-five Indian dudes?"

Connor shook his head and grinned. Faraz was growing on him for sure.

Faraz flexed in the mirror a few times then turned back to Connor. "Do you think I have a little boy chest?"

Justin opened the door and stuck his head in just in time. "There you are. Want a drink?"

Connor was already halfway out the door.

-

"To your first show." Justin held up his Solo cup and Connor squished his into it awkwardly. Then he nodded. "Let's walk."

It was late enough now that the first wave of goodbyes had happened; the initial after show intensity had worn off and the party mellowed out and segregated into zones. Everyone who was still hanging out was most likely in it for the duration. Connor knew most of the people still there, but they'd all had their moments with him by now, so he was more comfortable wandering from room to room without fear of being cornered and forced to listen to some story about that one time in junior high math class that he definitely didn't remember.

Justin and Connor headed through the kitchen, stepped carefully through the hole in the wall and walked out into the backyard. A large group was gathered by the hot tub now. Sarah and Nina, of all people, appeared to be demolishing Fragile Dave and Bailey at Beer Pong.

Connor and Justin approached but hung back on the periphery, watching with everyone else. Sarah sank a ridiculous shot, successfully ending Fragile Dave and Bailey's slim hopes of a miraculous comeback. She threw both hands up in victory as she and Nina screamed, bumped chests and pounded their beers.

Connor yelled to Justin, loud enough to be heard over everyone cheering, "Is Sarah wasted?"

Justin shook his head. "Can't get drunk. Side effect of the super strength. It's pretty awesome watching her drink grown men into oblivion though."

Nina pointed across the table at Fragile Dave and Bailey. "Rematch? Maybe you could make it a little more interesting this time."

Fragile Dave gave Nina the finger, then got to work resetting the cups.

Nina gave Sarah a million-kilowatt smile. "This is so crazy."

Sarah laughed. "What is?"

Nina took a sip. "I'm playing beer pong with the most kickass bassist I've ever seen in my life, who also just happens to play in my all-time favorite band—oh, by the way...I've decided that you guys are my all-time favorite band."

Sarah was genuinely touched. "Thank you. I don't ever take it lightly when someone says something like that to me. That's really cool."

Nina cringed. "Do you get that a lot?"

Sarah shrugged. "Not as much as you'd think. Especially with the whole super-secret underground rock band thing."

Nina squinted. "Yeah. What's the deal with that? I mean, don't get me wrong, I think it's awesome people have to find you and everything, but…"

Sarah took a long sip. "It's just better that way."

Nina nodded. That made sense through some bizarre filter of logic.

Sarah tilted her cup at Nina. "How did you hear about us in the first place?"

Nina's face darkened a little as the question landed harder than it should have. "Through Sam. He's Quikstuff's—sorry…that's what I call Connor—he's Connor's older brother. Or *was* Connor's older brother? I don't know what I'm supposed to say anymore."

Sarah's voice dropped. "What happened?"

Nina blinked and gazed off into the distance. "Connor's dad went out with Sam one morning and never came back. No one knows where they went, or what happened to them."

Sarah caught sight of Connor talking to Justin across the crowd. "I didn't know that."

Nina nodded. "I worried about him for a really long time. I swear, sometimes I wouldn't see him talk to anyone for an entire week. I didn't know if he would ever recover. Or if he even wanted to. People get broken, and then they start growing crooked and most times they just…stay crooked."

Sarah took a long drink and watched as Connor and Justin turned and headed back toward the hole in the wall. Nina's description sounded all too familiar.

Nina wiped her eyes with her sleeve. "But look at him now. Playing guitar. With Heatseeker. And he's actually good! You're gonna take care of him, right?"

Sarah nodded cautiously.

Fragile Dave and Bailey finished resetting their side of the table. Nina held her fist out to Sarah and waited for a bump. "Ready to take these chumps down, partner?"

Sarah bumped Nina's fist as she peeked over her shoulder, but Connor and Justin were already gone.

-

"Just because we're on the same team doesn't mean I won't kill you."

Alex was on the floor in front of the enormous bachelor-overcompensation flatscreen. He had a video game controller in his hands, and his mouth was stuffed full of chips. He was playing a split-screen shooter game—a multiplayer first-person infantry squad thing—with a group of stoned gamer kids. Connor and Justin ducked into the back of the room and watched the gameplay for a few seconds before Alex leaned over and yelled at the kid right next to him. "This is my therapy, so I don't hurt people in real life. Go sticky-grenade that carrier before I waste you myself." He dipped his hand into the enormous bowl in front of him in search of more chips, but he came up empty. So he handed the controller off to one of the kids next to him. "Going on a chip run. Twenty kills by the time I get back—I swear to God, don't test me."

Alex stood up, grabbed the bowl, and tiptoed through the maze of gamers. He geeked out when he saw Connor and Justin standing in the back of the room. He rushed over to them. "That TV is ridiculous. Gotta be the biggest one I've ever played on. Video games now, man…they're *insane*. Did I sound scary enough?"

Connor and Justin shared a confirming glance, then nodded in unison.

Alex smiled. "Sweet. I'm just saying all the stuff that Sarah usually yells at me. Hanging for a few?"

Justin shook his head. "Should probably head back to the living room to check on our stuff."

Alex nodded. "Cool. I'm gonna go look for some more chips. Or pretzels. Or maybe a microwave burrito. And a frozen pizza or something. Ooh. Maybe they have stuff for nachos. And a grilled cheese."

Connor and Justin walked back into the living room to see a tiny Asian kid behind Justin's drums, pantomiming like he was in the middle of a massive drum fill. Once the kid saw Connor and Justin, he scrambled off the throne to flee the scene, knocking over all the cymbal stands in the process. The kid dropped to his knees to sort out the mess he'd just made. He stared up at Connor and Justin, his cheeks bright red and scalding from embarrassment. "I'm so sorry."

Justin gave him an easy smile in return. "It's cool, my friend. No harm done."

Connor leaned down next to the kid and reached for the ride cymbal stand at the exact same moment the kid did.

Their forearms touched.

Connor's body started to tingle.

Something flashed in front of his eyes, and his vision went out for a second. His head hummed, like it was vibrating too fast, and the room felt like it was shifting under his feet. He closed his eyes to steady himself, but the feeling kept getting more intense. He fell onto his back, but he couldn't feel anything beneath him, as if he'd melted right through the floor and was free-falling in wide-open air.

The movement stopped abruptly. Connor was terrified of what he would see once he opened his eyes, but he forced himself to do it anyway.

He was standing in a bedroom, sometime in the past. A much younger version of the Asian boy sat on the bed; big crocodile tears streamed down his cheeks. There were towers of packed-up moving boxes stacked neatly all over the room. The boy's mom walked in. Connor's pulse raced so hard he could feel all the blood cells rush through his veins at the same time, but she brushed right passed him as if he wasn't even there.

She took a seat next to her son on the bed and wrapped her arms around him. "It's going to be okay, Drew. I promise."

The little boy collapsed into her and cried even harder. "Why can't dad come with us?"

A tidal wave of energy hit Connor from behind, hard enough to make his head buckle, and he was forced forward into—

A grade school. Little Drew walked the halls, looking scared. He was totally alone. The other kids stared at him innocently, out of curiosity, but it felt menacing, to Connor as much as to Drew.

Connor was swept forward again. This time into—

A different bedroom, filled with more boxes and an Older Drew. He wasn't crying quite as hard this time.

The visions were moving faster.

Another grade school. Drew sat by himself at lunch, and no one seemed to pay any extra attention to him this time. Connor didn't know which was worse.

Another bedroom and another Drew. This time he was unpacking—hanging posters of drummers and drum stuff on his walls. *Another school.* Now Drew was all by himself on the bleachers in gym class watching a group of boys play together and laugh. *Another bedroom, smaller than the rest.* Even more drum stuff on the walls. Drew was about to unpack something from a moving box but decided not to even bother.

Another school. Junior High. A big redneck shoved Drew to the ground and laughed as he walked by. It didn't even phase the boy anymore. He stood up, his face blank and locked tightly in survivor mode.

Another room. The last and smallest of all. There were two beds in it this time; one was for Drew, and one was for his mom. Drew's corner of the room was completely covered by pictures and posters of drummers. Drew sulked into the room with his mom nipping excitedly at his heels. She grinned and grabbed him by the shoulders. "I remember my first concert! You're gonna have so much fun!"

Drew didn't share her enthusiasm. "I can't believe you heard Mrs. Crozier talking to Cara and made her invite me. Do you know how embarrassing that is?"

She patted his head. "It's only embarrassing if you let yourself be embarrassed. And Cara seems like a really nice girl. Maybe you could even be friends. You need to make some friends this time. I got you something for tonight!" She pulled a plastic bag from under her bed and handed it to him. Drew looked at it dubiously and frowned. His mom was about to explode. "Open it!"

Drew open the bag. There was a brand-new Ramones t-shirt inside.

His mom plopped down on the bed next to him. "The man at the music store said people will love this band until the end of time and everyone will think you're super cool and know a ton about music when you wear it." She wrapped her arm around her son and stared at him in pure maternal wonder. "I just want you to have the best time tonight."

Despite his teenage angst, the gesture meant a lot to Drew. *Connor could see it as he—*

— came out of it. He was back in the living room as Justin and Drew stared down at him.

Drew was wearing the Ramones shirt.

Justin was visibly concerned. "Dude. You okay?"

Connor smiled at Drew oddly, with an uncomfortable level of familiarity. He scrambled up and led Justin away by the arm. He whisper-screamed excitedly. "I think it just happened!"

Justin looked confused. "What?"

Connor pointed at the tattoo on his wrist. "This. My power."

Justin's eyes went wide. "Seriously? What happened?"

Connor drifted away a little. "I touched that kid's arm, and then I saw things about him. His past. Him and his mom… moving from place to place."

Justin shook his head. "Just like Topper. It usually doesn't happen this fast. Sarah was right."

Connor was still buzzing. "Right about what?"

Justin leaned in. "Our powers get a charge from a normal show, right? Usually the bigger the crowd, the bigger the charge. But a house show, with everyone packed in super tight and stacked right on top of each other? That's a *massive* amount of energy. Like a supercharge. And I think it just kickstarted you. We should probably tell Sarah and Alex."

Connor grabbed Justin. "I'll find them. I need you to do something for me."

Justin shrugged. "Okay."

Connor nodded subtly toward Drew. "Go spend some time with my friend Drew over there and let him play your drums."

Justin nodded. "Easy enough."

Connor was about to run off to find Sarah and Alex, but first he spun back toward Drew and tapped him on the shoulder.

"Yeah?" Drew turned around nervously, worried he might still have a scolding coming for messing with the drums.

Connor just smiled at him instead. "Awesome shirt."

-

Connor was in no rush to find Sarah or Alex.

A few days ago he wouldn't have been able to imagine any scenario in which he was at a party, let alone this party, or having such a good time that he wanted to make sure he didn't miss experiencing a single second of it.

Which was how he ended up in the dining room.

He was headed back toward the kitchen when he heard the faint throb of heavy bass creeping through the walls and decided to investigate. He followed the sound all the way to the dining room, which thanks to someone's phone, a Bluetooth speaker, and an overhead dimmer switch, had become the de facto nightclub for the evening.

Connor had no idea what song was playing, a catchy, pulsating blast of brooding synthesizers, but it sounded incredible. He wished he knew who put it on so he could ask them to play it over and over and over again until it was burned into his brain and he'd never forget a single note. But he had just enough of a buzz going that he decided to jump-dance along with everyone else to however much was left instead. A few bounces was all it took to skyrocket his heart rate and make him dizzy in the best way possible, and he dropped onto his back on the carpeted floor. He lay there and took in big gulps of fresh air with a huge smile on his face while he watched everyone's shadows dance back and forth across the ceiling.

He felt someone sit next to him, close enough that it had to be intentional. He sat up. The first thing he noticed was her hair, bright blue; the second was that her arms were covered with tattoos, which probably meant she was way older than him. He racked his brain, trying to remember if he had seen her at the party at any point throughout the night.

Finally, she turned and looked at him.

Not only were they not the same age, but as far as Connor was concerned they might not even be the same species. She had dark skin and light eyes, and as the corner of her mouth crinkled up ever so slightly to give Connor a half-smile, he felt like his insides had just been hurled down from space. Then she stood up, turned around and reached her hand out to him, asking him to dance without ever saying a word.

He felt the firewall in his psyche try to engage immediately. He would never have thought that something as simple as someone reaching out for his hand could require such a vast amount of emotional courage until he was in the moment, and it did. But this was New Connor…Cool Connor…Guitar-Playing Connor. He didn't care how unbelievable anything was anymore.

So he took her hand and let himself absorb the sensation of her skin, lingering on its softness as she pulled him to his feet. She began to dance immediately, bypassing the few awkward seconds that could have happened while each of them waited for the other to start. Connor appreciated this greatly.

He watched her hips sway slowly to the new song that had just started, something slower and heavier with distorted vocals that made it sound ghostly and atmospheric. He tried his best to find the rhythm, but he was hopeless. So she put her left hand softly on his shoulder and her right on the small of his back. She pulled him closer and guided him, her body inches from his. He closed his eyes tightly as he floated in the dreamy tension he felt from simply being in her orbit.

Then she put her lips on his, and Connor Quikstadt had his first real kiss in the dark dining room of Faraz's dad's house while it was packed full of sweaty, recently-graduated high school kids.

His eyes stayed closed.

By the time he opened them up again, she was already leading him by the hand down the hallway. He could feel the heat radiating off her body from a few feet away. She glanced back at him and bit her lip. Every moment now came with a brand-new feeling that was somehow even better than the last. Connor had no idea where she was taking him. And he didn't care.

She quietly opened the last door all the way at the end of the hall, peeked into the vacant bedroom, and slipped inside.

Connor followed her in.

10

Connor woke up in a strange bed, with his shirt off. He rolled over and stared into the eyes of The Girl with Bright Blue Hair and his heart turned to cherry cola.

He wanted to ask her a million questions: how old was she, where did she live, what was her life like, and most importantly, when he could see her again? But she leaned across the pillow, gave him a quick kiss and slipped out from under the covers before he'd even had the chance to start.

As she stood up and stretched, he realized that she had his shirt on…and nothing else. All the blood immediately sprinted from his head. Now he had a super-official for-the-rest-of-his-life all-time favorite shirt. She peeled it off slowly, then tossed it over her shoulder as she bent down and retrieved her own clothes.

The longer Connor fumbled for the perfect thing to say, the more daunting it became. Before he knew it she was perched on the edge of the bed, lacing up her boots. She leaned down into him and gave him another kiss, but this time it was long and deep and perfect. Then she stood back up and waved a quick goodbye before she turned and disappeared through the door.

Connor knew he would hear the reverberation as the door clicked shut echoing through his brain for the rest of eternity.

So he did what any hopeless 18-year-old boy totally out of his mind with puppy love and no idea what to do about it would do.

He rolled over and screamed all his frustration out into the pillow.

-

The Girl with Bright Blue Hair stepped quietly out into the hallway. Justin leaned up against the wall, waiting for her. He gave her a nod of recognition. "If he ever finds out, it'll crush him."

There was a flash as Limo transformed from the Girl into a perfect replica of Justin, then stuck its tongue out at him—or, rather, at himself. Then it transformed back into Cool Old Biker form and followed Justin down the hallway.

A door creaked, just barely opening, and Sarah slipped out quickly in stealth mode, carrying her shoes and coat. She noticed Justin and Limo, and her face reddened for a split second before she was able to wrangle her composure.

Justin held his smile back a little, knowing there was more to the story. He nodded at Sarah. "Have a good night?"

Sarah unleashed her best death scowl, turned, and marched down the hall.

The door she'd slipped out of opened up again, and Faraz popped his head out. "Babygirl?" he called after her.

Sarah stopped dead in her tracks. Justin knew the exact face she was making without her even turning around: it was the look that held back a million gallons of boiling rage. But he couldn't help himself. "I think he's talking to you, Sarah."

Sarah forced herself to turn back, inch by excruciating inch. She stared daggers at Justin, ready to rip his head off multiple times as soon as she was given the chance.

Faraz blew her a kiss and whispered, "I miss you already," before he softly closed the door and disappeared back into his room.

Justin and Limo shared an amused glance.

Sarah strode forward and got in their faces. "I will END you."

They shrugged innocently and followed behind as she angry-stomped down the hall.

They passed the front room where Alex was still up playing video games while the band of leftover gamers were passed out on the floor all around him. Justin poked his head in. "Sleep?"

Alex kept his focus on whatever he was doing onscreen. "Little."

Justin frowned. "Coffee?"

Alex tossed the controller aside. "Now you're talkin'."

Justin used his free arm to sweep all the crumpled and abandoned red Solo cups off the kitchen table before he set the coffee pot down. Alex snatched it and immediately filled his mug. "Connor got his powers last night," Justin said.

Sarah leaned in. "Well, well, well. What's he got for us?"

Justin plopped down at the table. "He's a feeler, like Topper. He bumped into this kid and told me afterward he saw a bunch of random stuff from the kid's past. Didn't say if he picked up anything else, but I doubt he would have realized it anyway. He's wired from the last few days. Running on that new puppy energy. I sent him to tell you, but I guess something else got to him first." Justin nodded toward Limo.

Sarah shook her head. "Seriously? Like we don't have enough to worry about with him right now?"

Limo shrugged like its feelings were hurt.

Alex cringed and shivered. "I'll never understand how you do it…"

Limo transformed quickly into The Girl with Bright Blue Hair again and winked at Alex.

Alex almost choked on his coffee. "Counterpoint taken."

Then Limo transformed back into Cool Old Biker and crossed its arms triumphantly.

Sarah ignored them both. "A feeler doesn't help us much. Not today, and not down the line."

Justin reached for the coffee. "It takes time, Sarah. Topper helped us plenty."

Sarah whirled around on Justin. "Don't compare some kid we barely know to Topper. He might have pulled a rabbit out of his ass last night, but that doesn't change anything. That kid will never be Topper. So don't say it again."

Justin stared back, challenging her. "The kid is what we've got. Topper decided that. He saw something in him, and he made that call. So it's on us now. And we have to teach him. That's the only way this is gonna work."

Sara shook her head in frustration. "That's the problem. *None* of this works. It hasn't for a really long time, and we just keep pretending like somehow it's gonna get better. But it's not. And giving us a brand-new teenage liability with a learning curve doesn't change that. So I'm not gonna count on him to do anything more than get in my way. You wanna be his training wheels? You wanna go into this fight focusing on where he'll be every second, so he doesn't end up dead? That's on you. I'm perfectly fine to have him stand in the back and hold Alex's purse."

Alex yanked his t-shirt collar down, revealing a wide row of ugly blue and purple bruises that started at his shoulder and moved all the way down across his chest thanks to the energy blast he took last night. "Does this look like it's from a purse?"

Justin, Sarah, and Limo all squinted and stared. Justin shrugged. "Actually…"

Alex tugged his collar back up. "Ha ha. Doesn't anyone want to hear what I think?"

Justin and Sarah turned and said "No" in perfect unison.

Alex sulked. "Cool story, Mom and Dad. Guess I'll be in my room." He got up from the table, grabbed his coffee, stomped toward the living room but turned back immediately.

"You guys need to come out here."

-

Marissa was a sobbing mess on the couch. Nina knelt in front of her and tried to fight back the onslaught of tears with a crumpled tissue. Marissa sniffled and took in a few abbreviated gulps of air but showed no signs of slowing down.

Justin slid in next to Marissa and asked, "What's going on?" with just the right amount of comfort and concern in his voice, having perfected his tone from being in the same type of moment a hundred times before.

But Marissa was too choked up to speak. So Nina was the one who responded. "Her little brother Henry didn't come home last night. He was out with his friend Wade yesterday, and no one has heard from either of them since they left. Her mom is freaking out."

Henry and Wade…

Justin and Sarah locked eyes.

11

The van ride was silent while everyone thought about Henry and Wade. Connor hadn't been through everything the others had been through and hadn't seen all of the terrible things they'd seen, so he didn't know enough to know better yet. There was a large part of him that remained hopeful there were two 13-year-old boys still out there waiting to be saved. But he was where the hope ended.

For Sarah, Justin, Alex—and even Limo—all that was left to wonder about were the horrible specifics from the moment the boys were caught until their inevitable and gruesome end.

And nobody wanted to compare notes about that.

No matter where Connor went or how much he tried to help, he just felt like he was in the way. It was a feeling he knew especially well; it was cemented somewhere in his top-five most frequent feelings of all time. It was how he felt around Sam and Dad when they were all buddy-buddy talking music and guitars; it was how he felt at school. At outside places. In inside places. Pretty much anywhere where there were people, or animals, or anybody trying to accomplish anything. Last night was the first time in a very long time he'd felt like he belonged anywhere, but now suddenly that was gone, and the contrast was jarring.

So Connor just lagged back and watched the band members pick fights with each other as they wandered down the aisles of Peaslee Hardware looking for something that would help them kill a ten-foot-tall, six-hundred-pound Death Wolf. Connor knew they weren't actually mad at each other, that it was just displaced nerves from the thought of what was waiting for them in the woods. But that only made it worse.

Sarah waved a large butane torch in Alex's face as she yelled at him. "You can't just melt silver with a torch and make bullets; this isn't a horror movie, and it's not a werewolf. We don't need silver bullets. We just kill it until it's dead."

Alex yelled right back. "How could you possibly have any idea? It might regenerate, just like a werewolf. We might cut its head off, and then seven other heads grow in its place. You don't know. When there isn't one specific right answer, that means no answer can be specifically wrong, either—that's a basic principle of science. So what's the harm in trying? A bullet is always a bullet. It'll do damage. It might not kill it, but it'll definitely hurt it—I promise you. And besides, I know you've always wanted to make a silver bullet. You know how I know? Because everyone does! That's like freshman year stuff—monster fighting 101."

Sarah shoved the torch into his chest. "The only thing I really want is to not have to drive into my billionth spooky forest to hunt some terrifying thing that smells like death and wants to rip my throat out and chew my face off. But that's not going to happen, either. So put the stupid torch back."

Alex tossed his arms up in frustration and looked to Justin for back up.

Sarah shook her head. "Don't even start with the 'Sarah is being mean to me!' crap."

Justin stepped between them. "Alright…"

Connor figured this was the perfect time to wander away.

He stared at all the items neatly stocked in their specific places. He knew absolutely nothing about tools, so everything became a puzzle piece. How did that work? What was it for? How did you use it? He hoped he would stumble across the answer somehow just by wandering…that he would find something so intimidating and powerful, he'd just know that was it. He'd carry it back to them proudly, and they'd clap and cheer and tell him he was their champion, and that he'd just saved the day. But it was all just bolts and washers, light bulbs and extension cords, PVC pipes and three different types of chains wrapped around large spools—aisle upon aisle of stuff that all looked exactly the same to him. If Excalibur really was in there somewhere, he lacked the proper knowledge to find it.

So he walked around aimlessly for a few more minutes until Alex sprinted up, sent on a mission specifically to retrieve him. "You good, dude?"

Connor shrugged.

Alex motioned toward the front of the store. "Sarah and Justin are checking out. They wouldn't let me get the torch."

Connor tried his best to look bummed.

Alex turned, and Connor followed. "Where can we eat around here? Preferably somewhere we'll get the most food for the least money."

Connor stared at him. "Seriously?"

Alex grinned. "Consider this your first official Alex Frame life lesson: get as much food as you can every chance you get. It's a long time between meals somedays."

Connor shook his head. "No. I mean, how could you possibly be hungry right now with everything going on?"

Alex nodded. "First of all, I'm always hungry. And secondly, it's not just about the food; it's tradition. Gotta make time for Last Supper."

12

Topper and Justin had started Last Supper a long time ago, Alex explained. Back before Sarah and Alex. Back before Heatseeker. Back when they were a different band with a different name and different members. It was a way for them to freeze time and share a moment together, in case that was the last moment one of them had. The moment just before they were lost to the dark, for good and forever.

So Connor felt obliged to take them somewhere extraordinary and memorable, just in case. On paper it was a ridiculous decision, but for some inexplicable reason the idea grabbed ahold of him immediately and refused to let go.

When Connor was a kid, it had been called The Rainbow Roller Rink and was run by Dennis Grosso, an affable, happy-go-lucky family man in his 50's who insisted everyone call him Mr. G. Back then, it was bright and airy, decorated with a bunch of cheesy kid stuff painted on the walls, like clowns and balloons and rainbows—obviously. They had disco nights, an arcade, and couples skates and would send a card in the mail ever year on your birthday, good for a free cotton candy at the snack bar. When Mr. G died suddenly, everyone assumed the roller rink would die with him. But his kids kept it open and re-branded it, long before Connor realized that re-branding something was actually a thing that people did.

Mr. G had twins, a boy named Michael and a girl named Michelle, who not only seemed to be one another's only friend, but were also deeply connected by their mutual love of death metal. It was a logical rebellion given the backdrop of their upbringing, but in a town as small as Evergreen it seemed strange and dangerous, and made them stand out wherever they went. So the roller rink became their haven, and a tribute to the only things two they'd ever loved: their dad and heavy metal. They kept the skating but changed the name, and the once-upon-a-time Rainbow Roller Rink officially became The Dark Rainbow.

They blasted Mayhem and Dimmu Borgir during open skate. All the classic coin-operated arcade games like Donkey Kong and Galaga were replaced with first-person light-gun games where the common objective seemed to be shooting something until its head exploded, though they also kept the Pop-A-Shot Basketball machine for some unexplained reason. And they sold obscure metal t-shirts at the front counter, and built an enormous stage behind the rink, just in case Evergreen suddenly gave birth to a burgeoning thrash metal scene. Connor hadn't been inside in years, and there never seemed to be many cars in the parking lot when he passed by. But somehow, Mike and Michelle had managed to keep the doors open and the neon glowing. He guessed it was probably because of the snack bar.

Alex didn't say a word. He just stared in awe for the first few minutes after they walked in. "You look like you're about to cry," Justin teased.

"I don't think that's far from the truth," Connor replied.

Their signature item was The Dumptruck. For five bucks, customers got a massive plastic Tonka Truck (presumably cleaned and sanitized beforehand, but probably not), to be used at the nacho bar as a vessel to hold their heartburn-inducing, artery-clogging masterpiece. There were tortilla chips; unlimited liquid cheese from a hand pump; five different kinds of rapidly congealing meat; beans; guacamole; salsa; Pico de Gallo; and peppers that were roasted until they'd turned black. There were also fifteen different brands of hot sauce, and a wide assortment of lunch-sized bags of junk food chips to crumble on top for good measure, for anyone who was so inclined.

Alex was thoroughly captivated.

After his sixth full truck, he finally stopped.

He sat across the booth from Connor, in full bloat and caloric comatose, swaying back and forth slightly with his eyes closed. Connor was equally impressed and horrified by everything he'd just watched Alex eat.

They had the entire place to themselves, so there was no rush. It would be a few hours before it got dark, and none of them were in much of a hurry to get back out to McCaughan Woods anyway. Justin was the only one who rented skates. He did a couple of quick laps by himself, then sat down in the middle of the rink, laid on his back, stared up at the ceiling and watched the orchestrated light show.

Sarah picked through her pile of food disgustedly for a bit before she got up and wandered over to the video games. Connor guessed she would end up at the zombie slaughter game but was pleasantly surprised when she got some change and pumped quarters into the Pop-A-Shot machine instead. He'd played Pop-A-Shot with Sam when they were younger and eventually got good enough to beat him regularly and soundly, even though Sam complained about Connor shooting bank shots. It was funny how the rulebook never came out quite as fast as when the little brother finally started to beat his older brother at something competitive.

One of Sarah's shots went rogue. It bounced sharply off the rim, popped up off the plastic divider-slash-protector and caught her dead in the shoulder. It threw her off her rhythm, and she cursed loudly. She hunted down the wayward ball and furiously drop-kicked it across the rink. Connor shook his head but didn't allow himself to smile, for fear that she would somehow know. He glanced over at

Alex, who still had his eyes squeezed shut with his hands resting on his stomach. "Why is she so mad all the time?" Connor asked.

Alex sat up slightly and looked over at Sarah, who was back at it shooting baskets. "Because we're losing." He took a long sip of his soda. "You wouldn't know it to look at her, but Sarah is super competitive. She hates losing at anything. *Hates* it. But it's deeper than that. All of this is just…*poof*—slipping away. The jobs keep getting harder and more frequent. We used to do a couple gigs a month, but now it's non-stop, which either means there's a lot more trouble out there or a whole lot less of us fighting it. My guess is, it's probably a stellar combination of both. And it wears on you, man. It breaks you down inside. There's no way to do what we do and walk away whole. People dying. Kids dying. Losing friends. Losing Topper. You don't just…move on from that. When I first started, we were righteous. We had our cause—our purpose. We were the last line of defense, and we knew we were gonna win. Never doubted it for a second. And it's easy to feel like that when your heart is full. But then the cold starts creeping in, and everywhere I look now, it just keeps getting darker. My heart isn't full anymore. It's practically empty. But we pick ourselves up and carry on, even though we're losing pieces faster and faster, and it all just feels like a matter of time now."

Connor had tried his best to keep his head above water the last few days, but Alex had just dumped an entire ocean on top of him. "A matter of time until what?"

Alex dug out a chip, a straggler. "Until they win for good. And there's nothing left to fight for anymore."

Connor was incredulous. "Then what's the point of any of this?"

Alex shrugged and rubbed his eyes. He looked paper thin and weary. "What else are we supposed to do?"

They watched Sarah as she bricked a couple shots in a row, then spiked one of the basketballs into the ground.

Alex grinned. He didn't care if she saw him. "She'll come around on you. Just give her a minute. This is new for her, too."

Connor was confused. "What is?"

Alex took a pull on his straw. "Being the leader."

Connor shook his head. "Justin is definitely the leader."

Alex sighed sharply. "Thank you for completely disqualifying me from consideration. I appreciate your support. I told you, look like a kid forever and no one takes you seriously. Don't get me wrong; Justin is the best. But he's like the cool counselor in the summer camp movie who teaches you how to talk to girls and doesn't bust you when he catches you with beer. He's got your back, no matter what, and everyone needs as much of that as they can get. But there's a reason he's stayed alive as long as he has: when it comes time to make the hard choice, that's not Justin. He doesn't have it in him. Topper did. And now Sarah has to figure out if she does, too. Even if it is just delaying the inevitable. Even if she just became the captain of a ship that's already sinking."

13

The sun was still out by the time they got to McCaughan Woods, but it was already low enough for the shadows cast by the giant sequoias to stretch all the way down the access road and creep out past the entrance, as if the trees themselves were trying to escape.

Limo let his speed drop to a cautious 10 miles per hour. Sarah slid the side panel door open as the van glided along slowly, crunching gravel under its tires. She grabbed the edge of the door frame, leaned out and scanned the woods.

Alex scooted across the bench seat and stared out the window on the opposite side. He squinted hard, scrunched his face up super seriously and leaned in close to the glass. Limo hit a bump, and Alex tipped forward, smooshing his face against the window hard enough to knock his glasses off.

Connor almost laughed, until he remembered why they were out there in the first place. He dropped to the floor of the van and sat cross-legged, just to the right of Sarah. He made sure he was far enough away so there was no chance he'd accidentally bump her, but close enough that she had to know he was there, even though she didn't acknowledge him in the slightest. He tried anyway. "What are we looking for?"

It was such a long time before she responded that Connor had decided she wasn't going to. "You'll know it when you see it," she said finally.

It wasn't much longer before he did...and then wished immediately that he hadn't.

Two broken, crumpled bicycles, just off the road. There was a wide crimson path smeared across trampled brush and broken branches that led off into the woods behind them.

Sarah knocked hard twice on the roof of the van and Limo slowed to a stop. She hopped out and approached the bikes cautiously while her gaze swiveled in every direction. She gave the bikes a cursory glance, then tiptoed passed them and peered down the path, deeper into the woods.

She jogged back and leaned halfway into the van. "There's a trail…it probably dragged them behind it. This is where we start."

Limo killed the engine, and the sudden and complete absence of any noise in the woods made Connor's nerves go haywire. He wanted to run in the opposite direction and never stop. But he looked down at the broken bikes, and something inside him changed. He felt a sudden surge of white-hot anger that coursed through his veins.

Sarah ripped open the rear doors of the van and tossed out two plastic bags filled with all the goodies from the hardware store. She dragged a heavy black road case with *Heatseeker* spray painted in white along the side and let it drop to the ground with a loud thud. She pulled a retractable handle out of the top of the case, then lifted and tilted it slightly, until it rested on a pair of wheels built into the bottom. "Don't know exactly what we're gonna need, so we might as well bring it all." She looked at Connor. "This is you, FNG. Stay right behind us. Wheel the case. Understood?"

Connor nodded, and she held the handle out to him. He took it from her and pulled the case back and forth a few times to gauge its weight. It was heavy and full.

Alex and Justin dug through the plastic bags, stuffing their pockets with supplies. Sarah gave Limo a nod. "Scout it out?"

Cool Old Biker Limo nodded…then its skin went wavy again, and it transformed into a large, black-and-tan German Shepherd. Its entire body tensed momentarily before it took off like a rocket and sprinted into the woods.

Sarah looked from Justin to Alex to Connor to confirm they were ready, even though her face told them she wasn't entirely sure that she was ready herself. "Stay together. Listen for Limo. No hero stuff."

She didn't wait for a response before she turned and headed out, leading them all into the deep, dark woods.

-

They longer they walked, the worse it got.

The ground was dark and sticky, and there was so much blood Connor began to wonder how it could have only come from two teenage boys. He was immediately concerned by how little this rationale affected him. He couldn't help but think about everything Alex had said back at The Dark Rainbow, about how this wore on you and broke you down. He wondered if it had already started to.

The woods had gotten darker. The worse the path became, the slower they moved along it. It wasn't a decision they discussed or were even entirely conscious that they'd made. They just knew they were getting closer now, and each step forward felt like it took them further away from some invisible threshold of safety they would never make it back to. Eventually their deliberate hesitance started to work against them; it magnified every innocuous sound and hid a monster in every shadow, until their nerves were so frayed that only the tiniest thread remained.

There was a sudden burst of concerned barking a few hundred yards ahead. Sarah whipped around to confirm she wasn't the only one who heard it.

Alex locked eyes with her. "Limo. Gotta be."

Sarah had a far-off look in her eye as the veins in her neck bulged and her entire body coiled.

Justin knew what she was going to do before she did it. He reached out to grab for her. "No hero stuff, Sarah!"

But she took off, sprinting straight toward the barking. In a flash, she was gone.

Justin shook his head, then glared at Alex and Connor. "Fast as you can. Stay with me." They charged after her with Justin in the lead, Alex right behind and Connor already falling back.

Another *rat-a-tat* round of rapid barking rang through the woods, but it sounded different this time…it was wilder, frenzied. Desperate. And it made all the tiny hairs on the back of Connor's neck bristle.

He could barely see Alex in front of him; he didn't even want to think about what would happen if they got separated, so he pushed himself even harder to try and make up ground.

But the left wheel of the road case clipped a sharp rock jutting out of the muddy forest floor, and the case pitched wildly from side to side. The sudden violent shift in weight threw Connor's entire equilibrium off. He was forced to stop and steady himself to make sure he didn't fall over.

Limo had followed the blood just like they'd expected it to. Sarah had come running once Limo was trapped. Then Justin and Alex had fallen in mere seconds after Sarah.

Connor sprinted out from the cover of the woods into a wide-open clearing, then took a few confused steps and stopped. His band mates weren't anywhere to be seen.

Something was very wrong.

He caught sight of a shadow in his peripheral vision, a dark mass in the distance. It didn't move, but Connor could feel it as it watched him and sized him up. He forced himself to turn…something deep inside told him that he had to, that he would always have to from here on out, because this was who he was supposed to be now.

They were a few hundred yards away—the man from the party last night, still dressed in his black high-end designer suit, complete with a matching briefcase now, and next to him, a young woman with a flawless complexion and perfect hair. She looked intimidatingly athletic and was dressed head-to-toe in incredibly expensive-looking shiny black workout gear that was so form-fitting, Connor could see the curvature of her every muscle. They just stood there and grinned at him in a way that was so overly polite it felt maniacal.

The Suit raised one slender finger into the air and pointed down toward the ground.

Connor's eyes followed.

There was a steep, hollow ravine directly in front of him. The angle of the ground and the darkening sky made it almost impossible to see. He was so close, he would have fallen right in if had he taken another few steps. He tiptoed forward, leaned carefully over the edge and peered in. Sarah, Justin and Alex were all trapped down at the bottom, staring up at him. Limo, still in German Shepherd form, sprinted back and forth furiously and tried to climb the wall, but the angle was too severe. It just kept sliding back down. From what Connor could see, there was no possible way for them to get out on their own.

The Suit finally spoke, his voice slicing through the silence. "You're supposed to be down there with them."

Connor looked up across the open air between them. "Um… sorry?"

The Suit shrugged. "Doesn't matter. It's getting dark now. Our friend will find you soon enough."

Connor shivered.

The Suit knelt and thumbed through the numbered combination lock on his briefcase. "We've got something extra fun planned for your friends. You can watch."

Connor had zero interest in finding out what was inside the briefcase. He dropped the road case and scrambled back and forth along the edge of the ravine, looking for anything that might help his friends climb out.

Sarah yelled up as loud as she could. "The case! Push it down!"

Connor did some quick calculations in his head about the best way to do that but found no reasonable answer. "Bombs away…" he said nervously.

He heaved the case over the edge. Immediately, it went rogue and began to slam end-over-end. Connor winced with every thump. It was nearly at the bottom when its spine hit the wall of the ravine especially hard. It burst wide open, and all the weapons and secrets hidden inside spilled out. Sarah, Justin and Alex made a mad dash up the embankment and quickly filled their arms with as much gear as they could carry back down.

There was a soft double-click as the locks on the briefcase released. The Suit opened it and turned it toward the ravine, then backed away very quickly, as if he didn't want any part of what was inside.

Connor couldn't tell what it was at first…the ground looked like it was moving as it rippled in a way that made him feel queasy. Then he saw them. And once he had, he was sure he would never be able to unsee them for the rest of whatever was left of his life.

He counted six spiders, as big as basketballs, with translucent bodies. They scurried down the ravine wall frighteningly fast. The closest one launched itself into the air when it was ten feet from the ground and landed on a large boulder with a sickening *plop*. Its coloring changed immediately as it blended in with the rock, but when it parried off the side of the boulder down to the dirt floor of the ravine, its body remained the same, as if it was now made entirely out of the rock it had landed on.

Sarah didn't care what it was made of. She lunged forward and drove her fist down into the middle of its back.

Connor heard the spider's body crack, clear as a bell, but Sarah's knuckles were ripped open and gushing blood when she pulled them back. The spider took a few dazed steps, then buckled, done in by the fist-sized hole that went all the way through its broken, rock-covered body.

The punch had stung Sarah, too. She stared at her bloody hand and winced. She opened and closed her fist rapidly, trying to get some feeling back.

Another fat, translucent spider crawled out of the briefcase instantly, ready to take its dead friend's place. The five remaining spiders from the first wave all made it to the bottom of the ravine at the same moment. One crawled up a tree and immediately turned the same shade of deep, dry brown as the bark. Another skittered onto a small pile of gravel, and its body hardened and transformed, matching perfectly with the hundreds of different shades of streaked, dusty rock.

It suddenly became frighteningly obvious to Connor: whatever the spiders touched, they became.

He could feel The Suit and Workout Wear smiling at him. He looked up, and they both had big "we just put our feet up on your desk and what are you gonna do about it", grins on their faces. Connor swore to himself right then that he was going to figure out a way out of this, if only so he could knock every one of their stupid, perfect teeth out of their heads someday.

The Suit glanced up toward the sky and basked in the moment. "It's getting pretty dark out…it's going to kill you soon. And it'll hurt the entire time." Then he and Workout Wear gave Connor the same mock consolatory goodbye wave.

The Suit crouched down first. He stepped over the briefcase, lowered his right leg into it. Then he carefully gripped both sides of the frame and let his left leg drop in. It swallowed him up to his waist before he simply let go. He fell forward slightly and disappeared completely inside.

Workout Wear used a much simpler approach. She took a few measured steps and jumped straight up, folding her arms across her chest so they wouldn't scrape the sides on her way down. She slid right in and was gone in an instant.

Connor stared back down into the ravine and watched Sarah, Alex, Justin and German Shepherd Limo fall back together, ready to fight for their lives. This was the most terrified he had ever been, and the most helpless. They would hold their own for sure, but there was no doubt they'd be overwhelmed eventually. The current best-case scenario was that he'd still be alive to watch as it happened.

He scanned the rim of the ravine. Maybe he could work his way over to the other side, get the briefcase closed and then one of them would know what to do and—

The rational side of his brain yanked him back as Sarah screamed up at him, but he missed everything she said. He cupped his hands over his mouth and yelled back down. "What?"

She locked eyes with him. He could see how scared she was. He felt his heart crack.

She screamed again. "Back of the van! There's rope! GO!"

Connor took off and ran through the woods wildly, trying his best to retrace their steps. But he was led entirely by fear now—fear that he would never make it back in time, and fear that any second now he would hear the Death Wolf's heavy footsteps closing in right behind him. He looked up and realized he was no longer on any sort of path. He ran straight through the middle of the thick woods and cut between the trees, raising his arms just in time to protect his face from a row of low hanging branches.

He took two more steps after that. The first was directly into the middle of a shallow puddle that was filled with just enough water to soak his sock through instantly.

And the second was into nothing but open air.

Connor fell forward, with no earth to stop him. He kept falling faster and further, down into the darkness. He landed hard enough for all the air to be forced from his lungs.

He had a full three seconds to be completely and utterly terrified before the vision started.

14

It felt like he had been falling for forever.

Even though he'd never broken a single bone in his entire life, he could tell he'd broken both his legs the instant he hit the ground. Sam sat up and reached out toward the source of the pain instinctively. But wherever he was now was pitch black, and he couldn't see a thing.

He found his right thigh with his right hand, and his fingers inched their way down until he felt something sharp jutting out through a fresh tear in his jeans. *Tibia*, he thought. *It's bone coming through my skin.*

He worked his hand back up, slid it carefully into his right pocket and felt around for his phone. He turned on the flashlight, then held it out in front of him. Even though he'd only been down in the dark for a moment, the contrast in light was significant enough to sting his eyes and make him wince. It took him a few seconds to get acclimated.

He looked around as he propped himself up with his left hand and scooted back, careful not to move too fast for fear of stoking the searing, throbbing pain that reverberated in his legs. He appeared to be in some sort of underground cavern with dark, stone walls and a high ceiling, 20 feet or so above him, covered in heavy patches of creeping, crawling forest moss. In the middle of the ceiling was a circular hole where a tiny streak of the last few minutes of remaining daylight shone. The hole was just big enough for Sam to fall through—and, hopefully, big enough for him to climb back out of once he'd worked his way back up. *That* would be a very interesting problem to solve.

He hadn't fallen through the hole because of negligence or malfeasance. He'd been paying attention while he was walking and simply didn't see it. But it was his fault just the same.

He'd made Dad bring them out to McCaughan Woods earlier that morning (much too early, Dad had joked) in order to find one specific thing: the perfect piece of wood to finish the guitar. Dad had bought a beat up, vintage 1972 Hagstrom HIIN-OT guitar at a garage sale, and they'd been working on fixing it up together for the past few months. It had kind of become their thing, even though it was nothing but a mountain of frustration at first. They'd had a major breakthrough a few weeks ago, though, when they finally figured out the wiring…and suddenly there was actual sound when they plugged it in. The last hurdle that remained was the neck. It was missing a large chunk from the back, a "load-bearing chunk" as Dad liked to say, which made it feel like too much pressure on the fret board would snap the entire thing in half. So Sam had decided they should scour the woods to find the perfect piece of redwood to finish it. Something that was native and hundreds of years old.

Something that had seen things and had a history.

He and Dad had searched for hours, but the pieces they'd come across simply weren't good enough. Sam didn't know exactly what he was looking for. But he would know it when he saw it, and it had to be perfect.

Because the guitar had to be perfect before they gave it to Connor.

He couldn't wait to see the look on Connor's face when they told him it had always been meant for him. It was all Sam thought about. All the weekends he and Dad had sacrificed out in the garage, desperately trying every wiring hack they could find. Every night he'd spent hours scouring eBay and vintage guitar repair forums, searching for authentic replacement parts. Every time Mom had rolled her eyes at the idea of them ever actually getting the guitar to work. And especially every time Connor got gloomy and quiet because he thought they were intentionally excluding him—which, of course they were—when they'd sneak out to the garage together to work for another few hours.

All of that would be worth it the moment he saw Connor's face.

Sam shoved his phone into his mouth and held it in his teeth as he scooted forward on both hands toward the opening in the ceiling. The light from the flashlight bounced and swayed as he moved, casting magnificent shadows.

He stopped directly under the opening and peered up, looking for roots or hanging brush—anything he could use to climb back up.

He smelled it first.

A greasy, heavy wave of rotting, sickly-sweet air crept into his nostrils and coated the back of his throat.

A large, black mass moved quickly through the darkness behind him, but Sam never even saw it. He just felt a sudden, gentle tug right above his left arm, and then he shivered as the cool air touched his freshly exposed skin.

Sam looked down, and his entire shoulder was gone.

Waves of blood surged out through the severed muscle and tissue, cascaded down his body and pooled in the dirt. His initial reaction was that his feelings were hurt. He couldn't understand what he'd done to deserve to be brutalized like that.

There was movement overhead as someone ripped the brush away from the opening in the cavern ceiling. Sam couldn't see Dad's face; the light behind him was too bright. But he recognized the familiar shape of his father's head. He wanted to scream out, to tell him not to come down. That he should run away as fast as he could.

But when he opened his mouth to speak, no sound would come out.

It was getting harder to sit up. So he drooped onto his back and laid there, dying in the dirt.

He watched as Dad carefully worked his legs through the hole in the ceiling and lowered himself in until he felt comfortable enough to drop the rest of the way down to the ground. He rushed to Sam's side, terrified and concerned. Sam smiled, mostly because he loved his father and was glad he was there, but also because Dad looked like his feelings were hurt, too. Like he didn't understand what Sam could have done to deserve this, either.

Sam knew he would never get to see Connor's face when he got the guitar now, but that was okay. Dad would tell Connor it was Sam's idea all along. He knew that for sure. All he wanted was to close his eyes. And then, all he wanted was to stop breathing.

Dad was still watching over Sam when he died. He never even knew it was there…and he didn't feel it when it crept up behind him, opened its enormous mouth, sank its fangs in and ripped his throat out.

15

Connor came out of his vision. He was sitting on a pile of bones that used to be his brother and his father.

For the first time since they'd vanished, he knew exactly where they were.

A tidal wave of grief crashed down on him. He'd taken great care to protect the delicate sliver of hope he'd carried with him for the last five years; it was the only thing that kept him going—his hope that Sam and Dad weren't gone forever, that he wasn't permanently broken, and that they'd finally come home so his real life could begin again. But all that hope was gone now, and it was never coming back. That realization gutted him and exposed a vast and immediate emptiness inside.

He smelled it first, like Sam had. A greasy, heavy wave of rotting, sickly-sweet air crept in through his nostrils and coated the back of his throat.

Connor's fingers found a long, cool section of bone and wrapped around it instinctively. He stood up quickly, whirled around and scanned the darkness, searching for the Death Wolf. In every direction he turned there was another massive pile of bones, so many that he quickly lost track.

He felt it coming.

A large, black mass slid through the darkness behind him, and he turned to face it.

A low growl rumbled through the cavern. A warning. It surrounded him, as if it were somehow coming from every direction at once.

Connor felt his spine turn to ice.

He noticed something lying in the dirt on the other side of the cavern: a vintage, royal blue baseball hat, with the classic Mariners yellow pitchfork M logo.

Connor gripped the section of bone at both ends, lifted it high in the air and snapped it in half over his knee. He held a pointed shard in each hand, low at the hip like an old-fashioned gunslinger as he stared at the hat and forced himself to step forward.

He barely saw the Death Wolf as it exploded out of the darkness. It hit him with the force of a Mack Truck and drove him down to the ground and onto his back. Connor crossed his right arm protectively in front of his face a second before the Death Wolf's teeth ripped into his skin and sheared massive chunks of his forearm right off the bone.

Connor swung his left arm forward violently and slashed back and forth at the Death Wolf's ribs and arms. He stared in amazement as a six-inch gash opened and bloomed bright red blood through the matted black fur on the Death Wolf's right arm. Then its skin instantly stitched itself back together, and the wound disappeared. It had regenerated right in front of his eyes, fixing itself just like Justin could, and like Alex had guessed it might.

The Death Wolf locked its jaw on Connor's forearm, and the pressure built rapidly. Connor knew he only had a few more breaths before his ulna snapped. The Death Wolf would be completely through his arm and ready to start on his face. He stabbed at the

Death Wolf's head and felt the bone shard penetrate the skin slightly, but the monster didn't let up. So Connor brought the bone up and drove it down again and again and again, trying desperately to add some depth to the wound he created before it had the chance to heal itself.

He blinked hard as ribbons of his own blood dripped from the monster's frothing mouth and stung his eyes. He felt his arm about to give.

Then he lifted the bone shard up as high as he could and stabbed it down. It sank a few inches into the Death Wolf's scalp, then snapped in half. Connor watched helplessly as the top piece spiraled through the air and landed ten feet away. But the bottom half of the bone stuck, protruding awkwardly from the Death Wolf's head. Connor could see he'd broken cleanly through its skull and exposed a small patch of decaying, dark-gray brain matter underneath. He quickly jammed his finger through the crack in the skull and worked it into its brain. The soft tissue gave way easily and enveloped his finger as he pushed it further in.

Connor's body started to tingle as something flashed in front of his eyes and his vision blurred. His head hummed like it was vibrating too fast, and the entire cavern started to spin. He closed his eyes to steady himself, but the feeling just grew deeper and more intense.

The movement stopped abruptly, and Connor forced his eyes open. He was in—

A farmhouse kitchen. A litter of Golden Retriever puppies scampered around on the tile floor and chased each other. The smallest one, the runt, was having a very hard time keeping up. He tried to turn too fast, skidded out and slid into the refrigerator. A kindly, blue-haired old woman bent down, scooped the runt up and held him out to a very serious-looking gentleman. He gave the pup the once over then nodded an affirmative. It would do just fine.

Connor flashed forward into—

The man's car. The puppy was in a big box on the passenger seat with a fat blue ribbon tied around its neck.

He flashed again.

The man held out the puppy to a little boy. The boy squealed, grabbed the puppy and immediately started kissing it again and again. Connor couldn't remember seeing anyone so happy in his entire life.

He flashed again.

The boy and the puppy were both older. Bigger. They were asleep together in the boy's bed, snoring softly in unison.

He flashed again.

They were older and bigger still. Connor smiled as he watched them chase each other around the backyard.

He flashed again.

Now the puppy was in the backyard alone, forced to watch as the boy climbed the stairs and got on the school bus for the very first time as the man and his wife waved and took pictures. The little boy waved back and smiled at the puppy before he disappeared into the bus. The doors whooshed closed, and the puppy whimpered. As the bus pulled away the puppy dug frantically at the dirt under the fence until it created a gap just big enough for it to squeeze through. The man and the woman watched helplessly as the puppy sprinted after the bus. The puppy gave a valiant effort but lost major ground after just a few seconds. The bus made a right turn and quickly disappeared from sight. The puppy cut through the woods to try and catch up to the bus and his best friend in the entire world, the little boy.

Connor flashed again.

The puppy was in the woods all by itself. It was very dark now as it looked around, with no idea where to go.

He flashed again.

The puppy was a little bit older. Its fur was thick and matted as he watched it take small sips from a freezing cold stream. The puppy pawed through rocks and dirt, looking for something to eat. Its ribs were showing.

He flashed again.

It was bright and warm, and the sun was shining. The puppy chased a butterfly through a large field of brilliantly colored wildflowers until the butterfly got away. A rustling noise from somewhere behind it made the puppy stop, and its ears perked up at attention. It sniffed the air three times, then its lips peeled back in a snarl. It didn't like whatever was coming its way.

Two small, black shapes crept slowly toward the puppy. Their bodies were long and narrow, like worms, but they had many furry legs and blood-red eyes. They skittered in a circle around the puppy, flanking it as it let out a low growl as a warning. One of the worms shot through the brush and quickly wrapped itself around the puppy's body. The puppy rolled on the ground and thrashed wildly. Its jaws found the black worms head, and it bit down hard, tearing it open like an overripe piece of fruit. The puppy's teeth clamped down on the worm's brain and tugged hard, ripping it out of the worm's skull. The worm's red eyes faded out as its head lolled to the ground.

Then the second worm attacked. It encircled the puppy's throat and tightened viciously, choking the life out of it. The puppy's mouth opened wide as it frantically gasped for air. The worm crawled into the puppy's mouth, down its throat, and disappeared inside of it completely.

The puppy fell on its side and laid motionless and still. Its eyes tilted up toward the bright blue sky, though they saw nothing anymore.

Slowly, the puppy's fur began to turn black...

Connor flashed back to the cavern. It took him a moment to remember where he was, and that he was probably about to die.

He jammed his finger further into the Death Wolf's brain, determined not to let the gap in its skull heal. He tilted his face away to avoid a hot blast of the creature's rotting breath, noticing one of the many large piles of perfectly white, picked-clean bones. Connor dug his heels into the cavern floor, forced his right arm further into the Death Wolf's gaping maw, and coiled into his own body. Then he tilted his right hip down and pushed up and to the left with everything that he had. He forced the Death Wolf up and over, and its weight did the rest of the work, pulling it back down. They rolled across the ground together, locked and twisted in a bizarre embrace.

Connor pulled his finger from the monster's skull and reached desperately toward the nearest pile of bones. The tendons in his arm stretched beyond the point of no return and he felt them snap in an agonizing rhythm—one, two, three, four. His hand gripped a bone, and as he reeled it in greedily he caught a quick flash of the bone's previous owner: a beautiful Japanese girl who went for a solo hike one lazy Sunday morning because the cloud pattern looked particularly beautiful that day.

Connor smashed the bone down against the Death Wolf's skull.

Then he reached for another. It belonged to a teenage boy who had wandered into the woods to pick some wild black huckleberries for his first—and only—girlfriend, for her birthday.

Connor smashed it down, too.

He grabbed another. This one was from a middle-aged woman whose second husband insisted they go camping for their honeymoon. She'd hated it and resented him the entire time. Her very last thought was that her new husband had better get eaten, too.

Connor smashed it down.

Another. This one belonged to a girl Connor's age. He watched as the monster dragged her half-eaten but still breathing body out from the back of a red Subaru.

Connor smashed it down.

He reached for one more. It came from a five-year-old boy who was fishing with his dad and got swept away in the current. Miraculously, he was able to keep his head above the water long enough to escape the river once it slowed. But then he climbed up on the bank, passed out from exhaustion, and never opened his eyes again.

Connor smashed the little boy's scapula down especially hard, caving in a large chunk of the Death Wolf's skull just as his ulna finally cracked in half, and his entire right arm disappeared into the Death Wolf's mouth.

Momentarily freed, Connor dove off the Death Wolf and crawled away desperately. But with only one arm left at his disposal the Death Wolf was back on him in seconds. It flipped him over and pinned his legs under its massive form. Then it climbed on top of him slowly, wounded and angry. With nothing left to protect himself, Connor was forced to watch as it bit into his chest. Its jaw compressed, and he felt its teeth sink straight through the middle of his heart.

Connor reached up toward the hole in its head. His fingers found the cold, dead brain tissue, and he ripped out a chunk. Then another, and another. He kept tearing out pieces until he made enough space to work his hand between what was left of the brain and the monster's skull. He watched helplessly as the broken skin around the wound began to heal itself.

The Death Wolf bit down harder, and Connor whimpered. He knew he was going to die now, but he didn't care. All he wanted was to make it up to Sam and Dad. He wouldn't die with his heart breaking like they both did. He would die fighting.

He dug his fingers further into the Death Wolf's brain, grabbed hold, and pulled with all the force left in his arm and all the strength left in his body.

The Death Wolf's brain stem ripped free from its spinal cord with a soft, wet tearing. Connor watched the fire in its red eyes flash quickly to hurt and surprise before it slumped off him and slid down to the ground.

Connor held the brain in mid-air triumphantly for a few seconds before he squeezed it in his fist and watched pulpy, bloody chunks seep out between his fingers. He wished he could stand up, spike it like a game winning touchdown and scream, "Regenerate now, dickhead!" like they would have at the end of one of the terrible action movies he used to watch with Sam.

But he just laid on his back and gasped for air instead.

He was dimming out now, but that was okay. He didn't hurt anymore. He felt good, actually. Nice and fuzzy, like someone was placing a series of warmer and warmer blankets on top of him. And mentally he was fine with it, too. His life had meant something now, even if only at the end. No one else would lose their Sam or their Dad to that thing ever again, all because of him.

Connor smiled. He closed his eyes and his soft, shallow breathing stopped. The air in the cavern was heavy and quiet and the world got still.

Until something twitched in the dark.

16

Heatseeker was in a world of hurt.

Justin was sprawled out on his back, grappling with a large rock spider that had forced its way on top of him. He slashed at the spider's underbelly with a long barbecue fork, but the pointed tips bent back harmlessly, and he whipped it to the ground in frustration. The spider stabbed one of its front legs forward and punctured a hole through the soft flesh of Justin's cheek. Justin blinked in stung surprise, then grabbed for the leg before it could attack him again.

Sarah ripped the rock spider off Justin, broke its back over her knee and slammed it to the ground. The spider's legs skittered rapidly as it tried to flip itself back over before Alex eviscerated it with a blast of energy. Alex tossed another spent flare to the ground and stared at his charred, smoking hand.

Sarah helped Justin back up to his feet, took in a few big gulps of air and shook her head. "They don't stop." She was beyond exhausted and knew they were on the verge of defeat.

Justin reached out and steadied her. He tried his best to share whatever he had left, but it wasn't a whole lot. He knew they weren't much longer for the fight, but he did his best not to show it.

It was dark now, but their eyes darted around anyway, searching for the briefcase and preparing for the next round. There was an awful rustling sound, like a million pieces of paper tearing at once, as another spider spawned and crawled out. It scrambled back and forth along the lip of the ravine excitedly as it sized them up and waited for reinforcements.

A second spider started to creep out of the briefcase when the lid was suddenly slammed closed, trapping it inside and violently severing all eight of its legs. The briefcase was lifted off the ground then ripped and smashed into hundreds of tiny, splintered pieces.

The surviving spider didn't like whatever had just joined it at the top of the ravine. It tried to scamper away quickly before it was plucked up. It dangled helplessly for a few moments before something very large and very strong hurled it through the air. It splattered against the stone wall on the other side, then slid down slowly, a wide, wet trail of its guts streaking along behind it.

German Shepherd Limo stepped in front of Sarah, Justin and Alex, and arched its back aggressively. Then it lost its mind barking and snarling up into the dark.

The Death Wolf leapt down from above. Its massive form blocked out the moon. It rose to its feet and stood tall, its blood red eyes alive and piercing.

Alex sparked a flare, gripped the top, and charged up his right hand. Sarah grabbed a large, flat piece of limestone and cracked it in half. She held up one broken, pointy shard defiantly and handed Justin the other half. And German Shepherd Limo crouched even lower, ready to unleash hell at the first sign of attack. But the Death Wolf just stood and stared at them, watching and waiting.

And then it began to change.

Patches of black fur melted away to reveal hot pink skin underneath. The skin shimmered and pulsed out like ripples on a quiet pond as it rose up and pushed away from the bone. Then it changed color and shape, pulled back into itself quickly, and reattached.

Connor stood in front of them, half alive and barely breathing. He staggered forward, dropped to his knees, and collapsed onto the cold ravine floor.

17

Connor Quikstadt woke up in his older brother's bed, but the fact he woke up at all was the only thing that really mattered.

For as long as Sam had been gone, Connor never once thought to lay down on his bed. So even though he'd seen Sam's room before, a thousand times in a thousand ways, it felt like a completely brand-new place for the first few moments after he opened his eyes.

He stretched his arms above his head and gazed up at the trails of sunlight cutting across the ceiling. So much had changed since the last time he was in this room. He was barely the same person anymore.

He dug his elbows into Sam's sheets and felt the coarse flannel against his skin. He propped himself up and noticed a pair of legs stretched out on the ground, down at the foot of the bed, and followed them all the way up to Sarah. She was still asleep, sitting up but slumped over with her back against the bed. Her head drooped slightly to the side, and both fists were balled and ready in case she needed to protect him.

Connor tried to lay back down quietly but the creaky old mattress betrayed him.

Sarah jolted awake and sat up faster than she should have. She rubbed at her eyes with the backs of her hands and forced all the remaining sleep away. She stared up at Connor. "Hey."

He stared back. "Hey."

Sarah's head bobbed toward the huge Heatseeker logo drawing taped to the wall above the headboard. "Nice artwork."

Connor took in all the pictures, but this time through a very different set of eyes. "They're my brother Sam's. He drew them a long time ago."

Sarah nodded solemnly, then climbed up on the bed and sat down next to him. "Justin filled us in." She rested her index finger on his right forearm and lightly traced along the spider web of bright pink, deeply scarred skin that was still in the process of healing itself. "So you had yourself quite the time last night."

Connor swallowed, not entirely uncomfortable with the fact that she was touching his arm, but slightly nervous all the same. "You should see the other guy."

Sarah squeezed his hand for a moment and found his gaze. "We did." She sniffed the air and scrunched her nose. "Smells like someone is trying awfully hard to make breakfast."

Connor forced himself all the way up. "We'd better get out there before they burn down the kitchen."

Sarah looked around the room one more time, examining Sam's drawings again, as if she hadn't noticed just how beautiful they were until that exact moment. "Tell me about your brother sometime?"

Connor smiled, but the hurt crept in around the edges. Just like it always would. He nodded. "I'd like that."

When Connor and Sarah walked into the kitchen, Alex was at the stove with the two front burners going full-blast. He had a cast iron skillet heating on one and was seconds away from ladling big scoops of pancake batter into Connor's currently-smoldering and now permanently-deformed graduation present to himself: the dinosaur mold.

Alex's left hand rested in the flame of the other burner, to charge up his right. His logic, as he explained it, was to blast the top of the pancakes with energy to cook both sides at the same time, and therefore make them twice as fast.

After a lengthy lecture from Connor on the four basic principles of kitchen safety—including multiple threats of the fire extinguisher—they reached a shaky armistice: Alex would be allowed to make Connor breakfast without Connor's help, and Connor could tell Alex exactly what to do, as long as he remained physically seated at the kitchen table.

Justin poured the coffee. While they sat at the table and waited for pancakes, Connor tried his best to fill in all the gaps from the moment he left the ravine. He could remember fighting the Death Wolf, and up to the point when he died, but everything after that was blank, until he woke up in Sam's bed that morning. He got so lost wandering through his thoughts that he didn't realize Justin, Sarah and Cool Old Biker Limo were all staring at him. Based on the looks on their faces, they had been for quite some time.

Justin started. "Ready to talk about last night?"

Connor shook his head. "I thought I was dead."

Sarah finished a sip of coffee. "You certainly gave it your best shot."

Justin continued. "How did the whole you-becoming-a-Death-Wolf thing happen? Did it bite you?"

Connor smirked. "A bunch of times. But I don't think that's what did it."

Justin squinted, confused.

Connor ran his finger in a circle around the rim of his coffee cup. "I got a read from it while we were fighting: it used to be a dog…at least part of it was. Then it was attacked by this gross black worm-thing with red eyes, and I think that's what turned it into the Death Wolf. But I wasn't attacked by any worm-thing myself. At least not before I died."

Sarah's brow furrowed. "So what happened, then?"

Connor shrugged. "I don't know."

Justin talked it through. "You never saw it change form, right? It was always just the wolf?"

Connor nodded.

Justin chipped away. "So what else happened while you were fighting it? Did it do anything, like, crazy? Or magical?"

Connor thought back. "It regenerated. Like you."

Justin nodded toward Connor's arm. "And just like you too, apparently."

Limo tapped Sarah on the arm, mimed like it was going to shift, and pointed at Connor. Sarah stared at Connor, inspecting him. "So it didn't change form, but you did, right? And when you changed back from being the Death Wolf, it looked like when Limo shifts." She gave Connor a wicked grin. "Can you shapeshift?"

Connor shrugged. "I don't think so…"

Justin nodded excitedly. "Try."

Connor stared at him. "Sure. Um…how?"

Justin and Sarah locked eyes, and Sarah took a long, slow sip of her coffee as she thought about it. "Can you control your reads yet?"

Connor shook his head. "Not really. So far they just kind of… happen. But only when I'm touching whatever I read."

Sarah reached across the table, lifted Connor's arm and set it down on Justin's shoulder. She nodded at Connor, then toward Justin. "So shapeshift."

Alex walked over and dropped a tray of mutilated pancakes on the table. He slid into a seat and immediately locked in on Connor, because everyone else was. "Why are we staring at Connor?" he whispered, but Sarah angrily shushed him.

Connor looked from Sarah to Limo to Alex to Justin while butterflies fluttered in his stomach. He had no idea what to do. The Heatseeker logo tattooed on his left wrist caught his eye, and a calm cascaded over him and quieted everything inside.

He put all his focus on the tattoo and started to breathe, in and out and in and out. His body tingled, building up first in his fingertips, then flowing through his veins. His head hummed as he watched his left arm vibrate so fast it became blurry. His skin began to pull away from his bones. It freaked him out so badly his stomach lurched, and he had to squeeze his eyes shut to keep from throwing up.

The feeling started to softly dissipate, and as quickly as it came on it was suddenly gone. He took his arm off Justin's shoulder and set it on the table. He swayed back and forth involuntarily for a moment while he waited for his center of gravity to catch back up with him.

He opened his eyes, and everyone was staring at him.

Their expressions gave it away. He was different now, but not just his physical appearance or the fact that he'd shifted…he was also different inside. There was a power building in him, something far beyond anything he had ever considered himself capable of. He'd only felt it for a second, but he was already starving for more.

He looked down at his hands. They were Justin's.

The Actual Justin inspected him carefully, equally awed and creeped out. "So you *can* shapeshift."

Connor-Justin stared back, opened his mouth and responded in pitch perfect tone. "So you *can* shapeshift."

Alex pulled back from the table. "Dude!"

Connor-Justin turned his attention toward Alex, and a moment later, had become him. It was much faster than his first shift, as if he'd already gotten better at it. Connor-Alex grabbed for the tray of misshapen pancakes. "Cool story, bro. I'm starving!"

Sarah snorted and tried to hold her laughter back but failed miserably.

Alex glared at Sarah, then wheeled around on Connor-Alex, pseudo-offended. "First of all, how dare you."

But Connor-Alex had already moved on. He flashed quickly and became Sarah.

Alex instantly dropped his pretense. "Ooh…this should be good."

Connor-Sarah scrunched his-her face up and dropped his-her voice to sound tough. "People who say 'no pun intended' are cowards. Intend your puns, weaklings."

Alex lost it. Real Sarah scowled and cocked her arm back in an artificial threat, half-joking.

Connor-Sarah sat motionless for a moment, staring into space, then his-her body erupted and bulged out as it transformed into the enormous Death Wolf and growled at Sarah defiantly.

Alex nudged Limo. "Can you do that?" Limo slowly shook its head.

Connor flashed once more, and he was back to simply being Connor again. He gripped the edge of the table and steadied himself.

Justin shook his head. "So you're really, *really* good at that."

Connor tried to hold in his excitement, but he was practically beaming. Sarah stared at him. "You get Topper's badge and you can read like him. You have a moment with Limo, and now you can shapeshift. You fight the Death Wolf, and now you can regenerate and literally become it."

Connor was confused. "What do you mean 'have a moment with Limo'?"

Justin, Alex and Limo shared a quick concerned glance, but Sarah continued. She reached across the table and grasped Connor's arm. "You absorb powers. *That* is your power. Do you realize what this means?"

Connor shook his head. Her sudden unbridled excitement made him nervous about the answer.

She leaned back in her chair and smiled from ear to ear. She spoke delicately and savored the moment, as if she never believed she'd ever get the chance to say what she was about to say next. "We're going to win now. Because of you. Having you changes everything."

The enormity of that hit Connor like a house dropping on him. But that was nothing compared to what came next.

Sarah stood up from the table. "I can't wait to show you off."

Connor frowned. "To who?"

Sarah rested her hand on Justin's shoulder and gave it a triumphant squeeze. "To everyone. Pack your stuff. We're going home."

18

Connor finally knew the truth. Sam and Dad were dead.

Every time he thought about the flash he'd had in the pit, his stomach clenched. It was the closure he'd been seeking for the last five years, yet now that he had it, it was the last thing he wanted. No matter how dark it had gotten since they were gone, there was always a possibility—every possibility, in fact—that they were still out there somewhere, that they might make their way back home. That they would turn up on their own doorstep when least expected, and Connor would open the door and have his father and his brother back. He'd be able to shake off their missing time as nothing but a bad dream. Because that's what it had been; the worst dream—a nightmare he couldn't wake up from, from the minute they disappeared. Connor was all the way awake now though, and knowing the truth was so much worse than living with the mystery.

And there wasn't anything he could do about it.

It didn't take him long to go through his stuff. He didn't care about most of it, and the small collection he did want to bring fit pretty easily inside one of his Dad's gigantic old hockey bags.

The problem started when he got to Sam's room.

He'd been sitting in the middle of the floor for almost an hour now, but had yet to actually do anything. Justin and Alex had each come in to check on him a few times, and they were being cool about it. But Connor could sense an undercurrent of frustration building. He had no idea what he needed do. He just knew he had to do something, and he couldn't leave until he felt it was done.

When he asked what he should bring with him, Justin told him to pack like he was never coming back again. That was the first time it dawned on him that he really might never return. He'd barely made it through last night, and that was only 20 minutes away from his house. He had no idea what was in store for them now, what else was out there in the big, bad world, watching and waiting for its chance. It felt wrong to leave's Sam room as it was, in case he never made it back. He'd been the one looking after it all these years. It was only fair to see it through.

But it also felt wrong to change it.

Sam's room *was* Sam. It was all that was left of him now, beyond a shadow of a doubt. The way he'd hung his drawings. The order he'd stacked his records. How he'd crammed his socks into his sock drawer. All of the tiny, intricate details seemed so meaningful and significant now because they would never happen again. How could Connor possibly destroy that? It would be like Sam had never even existed. There wouldn't be anything left.

But that wasn't true. There would always be something left.

There were thousands of tiny pieces of Sam, buried deep inside of Connor. He'd carried them with him for the last five years, and he would continue to carry them, all the way until the end.

He started crying. Hot, heavy tears streaked out of his eyes, rolled off his cheeks and dripped onto the legs of his jeans. He sniffled hard and wiped his eyes on his sleeve. He knew if he didn't start doing something now, he never would. Eventually the carpet would grow up over him like moss and he'd suffocate, and that wasn't going to help anybody. So he decided that the first thing he saw as soon as he looked up was where he would begin.

It was the Hagstrom case, propped up against the wall, and half-hidden behind the dated, wooden entertainment cabinet Sam bought at the Salvation Army on 4th Street that had his TV, Playstation and record player on it. The guitar case was hard-shell and covered in beautiful, cracked dark-brown leather that gleamed when the light hit it just right. There was a three-digit combination lock on the side that made Connor freak out for a second, until he remembered Sam had made a specific point to explain what the combination was once. He knew this day was coming. Not the day when his younger brother would be packing up his stuff because he was no longer alive, but the day when the responsibility of looking after the Hagstrom and its case would be totally up to Connor.

The combination was Connor's birthday, April 19th: 4-1-9. It was an obvious choice; there was no way he'd forget it. But he also knew Sam well enough to give it more emotional credence than that.

Connor thumbed in the combination, popped the lock and opened the case. He ran his fingers through the plush soft-gray interior lining. He opened the small, rectangular "secret" compartment built into the case where the neck of the guitar would sit and saw there were a few guitar picks and a neatly rolled nylon strap. He stood up, let one end of the strap slip from his fingers and unrolled it all the way out. It was a Gibson strap, dark blue, with a white lightning bolt down the middle that made it look fast and cool and sexy and perfect.

Connor hung the strap loosely around his neck, reached up and plucked the Hagstrom off the wall. He lowered it carefully, then worked both the pegs on the guitar securely through their corresponding strap openings. He felt the weight of it tugging lightly on his left shoulder.

And then, he just let go.

The Hagstrom hung a few inches below his waist and rested softly on his right hip. It felt natural, as if he should have been walking around like this his entire life. He tilted the body up slightly to get a better look at the chunk missing in the neck.

At the exact same moment, Justin walked into the room. He let out a low wolf whistle. "Lookin' good!"

Connor's face flushed, caught in an intimate moment. He reached for the strap to yank the guitar off. But Justin hustled over and pressed his hand back down. "Don't you dare. Just came in for a progress report. I've seen a lot of guitars over the years…that one looks like it was made just for you."

Connor smiled, because he knew that it was.

Justin turned to head back out, but Connor called to him. "Hey, Justin?" He stopped in the threshold as Connor stared at the guitar. "Will you help me finish it?"

Justin nodded. "I'd be honored. And take your time in here. Seriously. No rush."

Connor took a deep breath. "Almost done. Just got one more thing I need to do."

-

It took him a while to get the hang of it.

One of his Dad's many endearing personality quirks was that he refused to buy name-brand office supplies, so all their paper, pens, scissors and tape had been purchased from his favorite local dollar store, The Dollar Jamboree. So all the tape Sam had used on his walls over the years had the double bonus of being really old *and* super cheap, which meant it didn't peel off easily.

Despite the setback, Connor was able to save all of Sam's drawings while only making minor superficial tears to the corners of two of them. Even though it felt like a ridiculous thing to take pride in, he raised his arms in the air all the same once he was finished, like a Wheaties box champion.

He tucked all of Sam's drawings into the guitar case, then carefully laid the Hagstrom on top of them before he closed the case and locked the lock. Then Connor stood up, took a great big breath, and looked around one last time. Even though this was his brother's room, it was without a doubt the room where he had grown up the most.

He noticed it as he reached up to flick off the lights on his way out and couldn't believe that he'd forgotten: the nail sticking out of the wall, waiting for the framed drawing to be hung back up on it.

The drawing that had started it all.

19

Mrs. Veseley answered after the third knock. This time Connor didn't hem and haw. He wrapped his arms around her and gave her the biggest hug he'd ever given anyone in his life. After a few seconds of stunned rigidness she let go and gave him a great big hug back. It made him happy in a way he'd forgotten that he could be.

He squeezed her even tighter, then let go and pulled away. He placed his hand on her shoulder and finally told her exactly what he'd wanted to say. "There were some days when you saved me."

Mrs. Veseley became a puddle. She blubbered a flash-flood of tears and had to brace herself against the doorway to calm down enough to catch her breath. Every time she would attempt to talk, the waterworks would start up again, and she'd hold up her index finger, imploring Connor to please give her a moment. But Connor didn't mind at all. She'd earned a million of his moments.

She eventually regained her composure enough to lean out, give him a quick kiss on the cheek, and mutter, "I'll go get Nina." Then she disappeared back into the house.

Nina strolled up to the door a few moments later with a very confused and slightly concerned expression on her face. She stared at Connor accusingly. "Dude, what did you do to my mom?"

Connor laughed. "I just said goodbye."

Nina nodded. "Aha. Taking off to start your awesome new life full of rock and roll adventures?"

Connor smiled. "Something like that. But I wanted to give you this first." He opened his book bag, pulled out Sam's framed drawing and held it out to her. "It was Sam's. I thought you'd like it."

Nina softened, touched. She reached out, gently accepted the frame and turned the picture around to get a better look. It was Sam's awesome complete-band live-shot Heatseeker drawing, but with a few minor additions. Connor had taped a picture of his face over Topper's body. It was his senior picture, which he'd obviously cut out of the yearbook. There was also a small scrap of paper taped to the glass that read, *For Nina. From Connor and Sam.*

Nina sniffled, looked up at Connor and laughed. "Man! What are you doing to the women in my family today?"

Connor smiled. "Keep an eye on my mom for me?"

Nina nodded. "Definitely."

She looked down at the drawing, then up at Connor one last time. "No offense, Quikstuff. But I kind of hope I never see you again."

Before he said goodbye, Connor stared at Nina hard and tried to remember every single detail about her, just in case she got her wish.

20

Connor had just turned ten the summer that he finally learned to swim. For whatever reason he'd been terrified of water as a kid. Some of it probably had to do with Sam forcing him to watch the last thirty minutes of *Jaws* one afternoon when he was six, but his mom swore it went back even further. She said he would scream his head off every time she'd even think about giving him a bath when he was a baby. So learning how to swim was never going to come easy.

They'd taken a family trip up to his Grandpa Frank's cabin on Lake Allison for a long weekend. Connor had been dreading it; the cabin was literally on the water, the front door a mere two hundred feet from the shoreline. He knew that swimming was going to be inevitable. So he'd brought along five brand-new Goosebumps books and pretended they were part of some mythical summer reading list he was getting a head-start on for school, hoping that his family would respect his scholastic aspirations enough to simply leave him alone. But no one bought it.

His Dad told him to change into his swim trunks the second they'd finished unpacking the car, and when Connor tried a Hail Mary by saying he'd forgotten to pack them, Dad countered that he could just swim without them since no one else was around anyway.

Resigned to his fate, he'd slunk off to the bathroom and killed as much time as possible, pretending to get changed, until Sam started pounding on the door incessantly and flushed him out of hiding.

It was the end of July, so at least the water was warm. Connor waded in up to his mid-calf and tried to look like he was having a blast. After a few minutes of gently trying to coax him in deeper, Sam and Dad shared a knowing glance and rushed him. They dragged him out into the middle of the lake and dropped him next to the floating dock.

Connor scrambled up onto it immediately. He yelled at them both and made a plethora of idle threats—he told them how much he hated them, and that he would never talk to either of them ever again—while they leisurely swam circles around him.

Eventually his Mom floated over and tried to coax him off the dock with a heartfelt apology and the promise of a personal escort back to shore. But he overplayed his hand, denying her repeatedly and exaggerating how badly his feelings were hurt until she'd said it was obvious he meant business, and she'd better just leave him alone.

He watched her swim all the way back to shore, get out and dry herself off. A few minutes later, Dad and Sam followed.

Connor figured this was their final gambit, the great big reverse psychology bluff. But after they disappeared into the cabin and hadn't come back a full ten minutes later, he knew he was in trouble.

He paced back and forth on the floating dock for a bit before his resolve finally broke and he screamed toward the shore. He begged for someone to come back out and help him swim in, but no one did.

Eventually his ten-year-old logic boiled over. They wanted him to swim? Fine. He'd swim. He'd jump off the stupid floating dock and drown, and they'd be sorry when he did. They'd never forgive themselves, and their entire lives would be ruined, all because they had the audacity to try and teach him to swim. He'd show them all.

And so he jumped off the dock—out of anger, out of spite, and out of the greatest possible motivator for any kid his age: one-hundred-percent pure boredom.

He hit the water hard and prepared himself to sink to the bottom like a stone, but his feet pressed down into the soft silt, and he realized he was able to stand comfortably with his head poking out a few inches above the surface.

The lake surrounding the floating dock was only four feet deep.

His family had played him perfectly. They'd tricked him, and they'd won. He had no choice now but to admit defeat, give in and fulfill the destiny they'd laid out for him by heading back to shore. He stepped carefully, getting used to the heavy drag that slowed his limbs as he pulled them through the water. His right foot landed on something cold, hard and sharp, and he freaked out, yanked his foot up and lost his balance. He lunged to the side and took four or five panicked strokes with his arms before he realized he was swimming.

Connor leaned back and let the water take him. He let go of all his nightmares about drowning, giant sharks and how many people had gone to the bathroom in the lake. He just floated. He allowed himself to be a kid on a warm summer afternoon with nowhere else to go and nothing else to do but enjoy the elegant weightlessness of it.

He was still swimming two hours later, doing large, lazy loops around the floating dock, when his Dad came out to start the grill for burgers and made him get out of the water.

A perfect summer afternoon when he was ten. That's where Connor's mind went once he realized he'd be leaving.

21

There wasn't a showing of *The Breakfast Club* anywhere in the entire 250-mile radius he searched online, so Connor had no idea what he was going to do…until he remembered about The Hudson.

The Hudson was a small, four-screen revival theater near the University of Northwestern Washington, just off-campus. A few nights a week they did something called Flashback Cinema, where they would screen classic movies from the '60s, '70s, '80s and '90s. That night, they just so happened to be showing *Uncle Buck* at 8:30 PM. While it wasn't *The Breakfast Club*, Connor figured it would do just fine. His dad always told him there was a little bit of magic in every John Hughes movie. Plus, he distinctly remembered them all watching it together as a family after Thanksgiving dinner one year, and his mom had lost it during the part where U.B. met with the assistant principal trying to smother his niece's creativity, gave her a quarter, and told her to go downtown and have a rat gnaw the giant wart off her face.

Even though Connor knew where they were going when they left his house, he still wasn't ready by the time the van pulled up in front of the theater. He held his mom's hand and helped her climb out. He couldn't believe how light and weak it felt, like there weren't even bones within. She was frighteningly skinny, and every breath she took looked like a monumental chore. But he couldn't just leave her in her room. He owed her more than that—a chance, at least. What she did with it was totally up to her. So he'd brought her to The Hudson, banking on the fact that John Hughes, John Candy and some peanut butter cups might spark enough hope to guide her out of the despondent cloud she'd lost herself in so many years ago.

He went to the window and bought her a ticket, then stuffed all the remaining money he had in the world into her front jacket pocket. A soft, cool breeze passed by, and she shivered. Connor zipped her jacket up and tried to catch her eye, but she just kept staring off into space.

He felt a flare of anger spark deep in his gut. He'd eaten a lot of hurt over the years, and now it was fighting its way to the surface. So he let it all out, since this might have been his last chance. And because he had to.

He put his hands on the sides of her face and forced her to look at him. "Mom, they're gone. Sam and Dad—I found them. They aren't coming back. But it's not because they didn't want to; it's because they couldn't. They disappeared from both our lives, you know—they left us both. But I never got to break down because you did it first. And then I had to hold it together while *you* left me, too. I was alone for a really long time. But I'm not alone anymore. I'm leaving, Mom. I have to. I'm doing this out of hope that it'll help you, and because I don't know what else to do." His anger melted to grief, for her and for himself. For a future where they were together and still had each other to depend on. A future that would never exist.

He stared at her, and for the first time in five years he swore he saw a glimmer of light in her eyes. A large, solitary tear streaked down her cheek and she softly croaked, "That's nice, Connor."

He leaned in and kissed her gently on the top of her head. "Nina and her mom will pick you up after the movie. I love you."

Then he turned and walked away. He had to leave her now, just like she had left him.

They were waiting outside the van. Sarah wrapped an arm around him, and he leaned into her. "People don't get the goodbyes they deserve. We've seen a lot of them, and that's the truth. They're basic. And sad. What you just got is better than most. Even if it doesn't feel like it."

Connor sniffled and nodded like he understood. Maybe he would recognize that someday, after he'd seen enough other goodbyes of his own.

He watched his mom on the sidewalk. She looked so little and alone, but that didn't change the fact he had to go. He wondered if this was how she'd felt the first time she'd left him at school. For a second he wanted to run up and ask her.

Sarah reached into the van and dug through the pocket on the back of the front passenger seat. She pulled out a beat-up old atlas and held it out to Connor. "Feel like sitting up front and navigating? There's this whole gigantic world out there you might like to see."

Connor stared at the atlas. "You know there's a GPS on every single phone in existence now, right?"

Alex rolled his eyes at Sarah. "Also, the scenery is essentially the same while looking out any one of the many, many windows in the van."

Sarah shoved Alex. "Shut up. And the atlas is symbolic. It's a gesture." She forced Connor to take it. "So get on up there, Quikstuff. And lead us to where we're going."

Connor climbed into the front passenger seat, shaking his head. He hadn't lost "Quikstuff" just yet. He figured he'd pretend like it bothered him for a while.

He turned around and watched Alex, Sarah and Justin get in back. "Speaking of which, where are we going?"

Justin smiled. "A safe haven in the Midwest that wears its heart proudly on its frozen parka sleeve. A refuge protected by the Mighty Mississippi and the sound and fury of loud guitars."

Alex shook his head. "Cool story, Justin. But calm down."

Sarah gently took the atlas from Connor and flipped through pages. "It's time for your grand introduction. We're taking you home to meet the rest of underground." She held the atlas open to the map of the entire country and tapped her finger on the border between Wisconsin and Minnesota.

Connor leaned forward and squinted. "What am I looking for, here? I don't see anything."

Sarah smiled. "You will. Soon enough.

Connor didn't know much about Wisconsin or Minnesota aside from cheese and hockey, but he figured he'd have more than enough time to get filled in on the drive.

Cool Old Biker Limo climbed up into the driver's seat and slammed the door shut as Connor stared out at his mom. She just stood there, looking lost. He reached for the door, but Limo grabbed him first. It dug into the pocket of its leather jacket, fished something out and held it up to Connor. It was an old photograph from when Connor was younger: he and Sam and Mom and Dad, all holding sparklers on a bright, sunny afternoon at some Fourth of July cookout.

Limo pointed to Connor's dad, then looked at Connor for confirmation. It took him a second to realize what Limo was getting at. "Yeah. That's my dad. Why?"

Limo was quiet as it stared at the picture and concentrated. Then it began to change slowly, in tiny sections. It was different than what Connor had seen in its previous changes, as if it was much harder this time. Limo ducked out of the van again just as the transformation finished.

Connor lunged forward and pressed himself against the windshield. He could feel his sanity teetering above some bottomless abyss as he suddenly watched his father walk toward his mother as if they were two regular people meeting up for a regular date at the regular movies. He wanted so badly for it to be true that there was a part of him that was willing to let go, to jump into the abyss with them and never look back.

Then Sarah leaned up and squeezed his arm, as if she knew exactly what he was thinking. The gesture steeled him and gently tugged him back to reality. It wasn't really his dad. It wasn't even his mom anymore. Not really.

But when she saw Limo in his shifted shape, she was herself again. Her blank stone facade cracked open, and a burst of recognition shone right through. She rushed him, wrapped her arms around him, buried her face in his chest and sobbed so hard her body convulsed.

It was too much and too hard, so Connor forced himself to look away.

Justin leaned in and caught his eye. "You okay?"

Connor shook his head. "No. But I will be. Someday."

Sarah handed Connor the atlas. "Ready?"

Connor nodded. "Almost."

He reached down to find his book bag, unzipped the pocket, and pulled out his melted, deformed graduation present to himself: the dinosaur pancake mold. There was a piece of string hooked around the top. He reached up, tied it around the rearview mirror and let it dangle as he admired it. "So I can make us pancakes wherever we go."

Alex held his fist out, and Connor bumped it. Then he stared over Connor's shoulder and made a serious stink-face. "Gross. Don't look. For real."

Connor looked back through the windshield. His Mom and Limo/Dad were in the middle of an incredibly deep and slobbery kiss. He flinched. "At what point does this become disturbing?"

Alex leaned in. "About five minutes ago. Especially once you realize that Limo has now made out with both you *and* your mom."

"Dude!" Sarah said angrily.

"What?" Alex suddenly realized his mistake, but it was too late to take it back.

Connor whipped around in the front seat, confused as hell. "I never made out with Limo…"

Sarah, Justin and Alex all dodged his gaze.

Connor stared at his band and waited for an answer.

His memory finally kicked in, and his cheeks flushed bright red. "WHAT THE FUCK?!?"

ACKNOWLEDGEMENTS

If I had one wish for every person on Earth it would be that they all had someone who believes in them as much as my wife believes in me. None of this would have happened without her and I'll never be able to thank her enough. All the best things in my life are because of you.

My kids changed my entire world. They helped me rediscover the best parts of my imagination and unleash all the ridiculous things inside. Writing a book is cool, but being your dad is a million times cooler.

I come from a family of musicians and storytellers so it's absolutely no coincidence that music is at the heart of the most important story I've ever tried to tell. Thank you all for loving me, encouraging me, and never making me feel foolish for chasing a dream.

An enormous thank you to Steven Luna for his wisdom, patience, artwork and editing. Whatever elements of this story you liked the best they were no doubt improved by his hand.

Thank you to Clayton Smith for making everything look nice and professional inside and swapping stories over gigantic sandwiches.

It took me a lot longer than I thought it would to get to the point where I'm sitting in my kitchen thinking about what exactly I should write for this page, but looking back down now from the top of the mountain it was so incredibly worth it. So write the book. Start the band. Take the trip. If you spend your time wondering about something, do it. Because It all goes by so fast.

Thank you for taking the time to read this book. You have no idea how much it means to me.

See you in the next one.

Made in United States
Orlando, FL
21 February 2022